THE
DESERT KING'S
CAPTIVE BRIDE

BY
ANNIE WEST

First Published in Great Britain 2017
By Mills & Boon, an imprint of HarperCollins*Publishers*
1 London Bridge Street, London, SE1 9GF

© 2017 Annie West

ISBN: 978-0-263-92414-5

Our policy is to use papers that are natural, renewable and recyclable
products and made from wood grown in sustainable forests. The logging
and manufacturing processes conform to the legal environmental
regulations of the country of origin.

Printed and bound in Spain
by CPI, Barcelona

Growing up near the beach, **Annie West** spent lots of time observing tall, burnished lifeguards—early research! Now she spends her days fantasising about gorgeous men and their love lives. Annie has been a reader all her life. She also loves travel, long walks, good company and great food. You can contact her at annie@annie-west.com or via PO Box 1041, Warners Bay, NSW 2282, Australia.

Visit the Author Profile page
at millsandboon.co.uk for more titles.

For my darling Dad

CHAPTER ONE

THE STEWARDESS STOOD ASIDE, inviting her to leave the plane. Ghizlan stood, smoothing her moss-green tailored skirt and jacket with a hand that barely trembled.

She'd had days to prepare herself. Days to learn to mask the shock and, yes, grief. She'd never been close to her father, a distant man, more interested in his country than his daughters, yet his sudden death at fifty-three from a brain aneurism had rocked the foundations of her world.

Ghizlan drew herself up, donning the polite smile her father had deemed appropriate for a princess, and, with a murmur of thanks to the staff, stepped out of the aircraft.

A cool evening wind whipped down off the mountains, eddying around her stockinged legs. Briefly she pondered how nice it must be to travel in comfortable, casual clothes, before letting the idle thought tear free on a gust of air. She was the daughter of a royal sheikh. She didn't have that freedom.

Setting her shoulders, she gripped the rail and descended the stairs to the tarmac, aware that her legs were unsteady.

Falling flat on her face wasn't an option. Clumsiness had never been allowed and now, more than ever, it was imperative she look calm. Until her father's heir was named she was the country's figurehead, a face the people knew. They would rely on her, eldest daughter of their revered Sheikh, to ensure the smooth running of matters while his successor was confirmed.

Who that would be, Ghizlan didn't know. Her father had been negotiating a new marriage when he died, still hoping to get that all-important male heir.

She reached the tarmac and paused. On three sides rose the mountains, purple in the late afternoon, surrounding the capital on its plateau. Behind her on the fourth side the mountain dropped abruptly to the Great Sand Desert.

Ghizlan breathed deeply. Despite the grave circumstances of her arrival in Jeirut, her heart leapt at the familiar scents of clear mountain air and spices that even airline fuel couldn't quite eradicate.

'My lady.' Azim, her father's chamberlain, hurried towards her, face drawn and hands twisting.

Ghizlan quickly crossed to the old man. If anyone could claim intimacy with her father it was Azim, his right-hand man for years.

'Welcome, my lady. It's a relief to have you back.'

'It's good to see you, Azim.' Ignoring custom, Ghizlan reached for his hands, holding them in hers. Neither of them would ever admit it but she had been closer to Azim than to her father.

'Highness!' He darted a worried look to one side where soldiers guarded the perimeter of the airstrip.

Ghizlan ignored them. 'Azim? How are you?' She knew her father's death must have been a terrible blow to him. Together they'd made it their lives' work to bring Jeirut into the new millennium by a combination of savvy negotiation, insightful reform and sheer iron will.

'I'm well, my lady. But it's I who should be asking...' He paused, gathering himself. 'I'm sorry for your loss. Your father wasn't merely a visionary leader, he was the mainstay of our democracy and a protector to you and your sister.'

Ghizlan nodded, releasing Azim's hands and moving towards the terminal. Her father had been all those things, but her country's democratic constitution would continue after his death. As for her and Mina, they'd learned long ago not to expect personal support from their father. Instead they were used to being paraded as role models for education, the rights of women and other causes. He might have been a visionary who'd be remembered as a great man, but the sad truth was neither she nor her younger sister could be heartbroken at his passing.

She shivered, knowing she should feel more.

As they approached the terminal Azim spoke again. 'My lady, I have to tell you…' He paused as some soldiers marched forward.

'Wait. My lady.' His voice was barely above a whisper and Ghizlan stopped, attuned to the urgency radiating from him. 'I need to warn you—'

'My lady.' A uniformed officer bowed before her. 'I'm here to escort you to the Palace of the Winds.'

Ghizlan didn't recognise him, a tough-looking man in his thirties, though he wore the uniform of the Palace Guard. But then she'd been away more than a month and military transfers happened all the time.

'Thank you, but my own bodyguard is sufficient.' She turned but to her surprise couldn't see her close personal protection officers.

As if reading her mind the captain spoke again. 'I believe your men are still busy at the plane. There are new regulations regarding baggage checks. But that needn't delay you.' He bowed again. 'My men can escort you. No doubt you are eager to see the Princess Mina.'

Ghizlan blinked. No palace employee would dream of commenting on the intentions of a member of the royal family. This man *was* new. But he was right. She'd fretted over how long it had taken to get back to Jeirut. She hated the idea of Mina all alone.

Again she turned but couldn't see her staff. It went against every instinct to leave them, but now, finally in Jeirut, her worry over Mina had grown to something like panic. Ghizlan hadn't been able to reach her by phone since yesterday. Her sister was only seventeen, just finished school. How had she coped with their father's death?

Only men attended Jeiruti funerals, even state funerals, but Ghizlan had wanted to be here to take the burden of the other formalities, receiving the respects of provincial sheikhs and the royal court. But tradition had prevailed and her father had been interred within the requisite three days while Ghizlan had been stuck on another continent.

'Thank you. I appreciate it.' She turned to Azim. 'Would you mind explaining that I've gone on to the palace and that I'm in safe hands?'

'But, my lady...' Azim darted a glance towards the guards surrounding them. 'I need to speak with you in private. It's crucial.'

'Of course. There are urgent matters to discuss.' Her father's death was a constitutional nightmare. With no clear heir to the sheikhdom, it could take weeks to decide his successor. Ghizlan felt the weight of responsibility crush down on her shoulders. She, as a woman, couldn't succeed, but she'd have a key role in maintaining stability until the succession was finalised. 'Give me two hours then we'll meet.'

She nodded to the captain of the guards to proceed.

'But, my lady—' Azim fell silent as the captain stepped towards him, deliberately invading the old man's space, expression stern and body language belligerent.

Ghizlan fixed the officer with a stare she'd learned from her father. 'If you're going to work for the palace you need to learn the difference between attentiveness and intimidation.' The guard's eyes met hers, widening in surprise. 'This man is a valued aide. I expect him, and everyone else approaching me, to be treated with respect. Is that understood?'

The officer nodded and stepped away. 'Of course, my lady.'

Ghizlan wanted to take Azim's hands once more. He

looked old and frail. But she desperately needed to see Mina. Instead she smiled gently. 'I'll see you soon and we can discuss everything.'

'Thank you for your escort.' Ghizlan stopped in the vast palace atrium. 'However, in future, there's no need for you or your men to come within the palace itself.' The security arrangements didn't include armed men in the corridors.

The captain bowed, the slightest of inclines. 'I'm afraid I have orders to the contrary, my lady. If you'll come with me?'

'Orders?' Ghizlan stared. The man might be new but he overstepped the mark. 'Until my father's successor is announced *I* give the orders in the palace.'

The man's expression didn't alter.

Ghizlan was used to soldiers. Protecting the royal family was a prestigious rung on the military career ladder, but never had she met one like this. He looked back, fixed on a point near her ear, his expression wooden.

'What's going on here?' Ghizlan kept her tone calm, despite the unease trickling, ice cold, down her spine. She hadn't paid attention before, had been too lost in her thoughts to notice, but a quick glance revealed all the guards were unfamiliar. One new face, maybe two, was possible. But this...

'My orders are to take you to the Sheikh's office.'

'My father's office?' Despite a lifetime's training in poise, Ghizlan couldn't prevent the hammer of her heart against her ribs, or the way her hand fluttered up as if to stop it. An instant later she'd controlled the gesture, forcing her hand down. 'Who gave this order?'

The captain didn't speak, but gestured for her to precede him.

From confusion and shock, anger rose. Whatever was going on, she deserved answers and she intended to get them! She strode forward, only to slam to a halt as the whole squad of guards moved with her.

Slowly she spoke, articulating each word precisely. She didn't bother to turn her head. 'Dismiss your men, Captain. They are neither required nor welcome in this place.' For the beat of her pulse, then another she waited. 'Unless you feel unable to guard a solitary woman?'

Ghizlan didn't deign to wait for his response, but strode away, her high heels smacking the marble floor, fire fizzing in her veins. It should have been a relief to hear the men moving away in the opposite direction, except she knew their officer followed right behind her.

Something was very, very wrong. The knowledge twisted her insides and raised the hair at the nape of her neck.

Ignoring a lifetime's training, Ghizlan didn't bother knocking on the door to the royal office, but thrust it open, barely pausing in her stride.

Her breath escaped in a rush of frustration as she surveyed the room. It was empty. The person who'd allegedly given such outrageous orders to the palace guard, if it *was* the palace guard, was nowhere to be seen.

She swayed to a halt before the vast desk and her heart spasmed as she inhaled the faint, familiar scents of papers and sandalwood, as well as spearmint from the chews her father kept in a box on his desk.

Time wound back and she could almost believe it all a nightmare. That her father would enter from the rear door to his private quarters, intent on some report or new scheme to help his people.

Ghizlan planted her palms on the satiny wood of the desk and drew in a deep breath. She had to get a grip.

Whatever was going on, and instinct belatedly warned her something was, her father was gone.

A shudder racked her so hard she had to grit her teeth so they didn't chatter. She'd known all her life that her father's love was for his country not his children. Yet he'd been vigorous enough to contemplate a third marriage. It still seemed impossible—

Ghizlan straightened. She didn't have time to wallow in sentiment. She needed to discover what was happening. For it had seemed as if the guards kept her prisoner rather than protected her. Unease stirred again.

She smoothed her palms down her skirt, twitched her jacket in place and pushed her shoulders back, ready to face whatever unpalatable situation awaited.

She was halfway to the study's rear door when a voice stopped her. It wasn't loud but the deep, bass rumble cut through her jumbled thoughts like the echo of mountain thunder.

'Princess Ghizlan.'

She swung around, twisting on a stiletto heel. Her pulse tripped unevenly as she took in the great bear of a man standing before the closed door through which she'd entered.

He towered over her even though she wore heels and was often described as statuesque. The disparity in their heights surprised her. He wasn't just tall, he was wide across the shoulders, his chest deep and his legs long and heavily muscled.

He wore a horseman's clothes—a pale shirt and trousers tucked into long leather boots. A cloak was pushed back off his shoulders so she glimpsed the knife at his waist. Not a decorated, ceremonial dagger as her father had worn from time to time, but a plain weapon, its handle gleaming with the patina of use.

'Weapons aren't permitted in the palace,' she snapped out. It was easier to concentrate on that than the strangely heavy thud of her pulse as she met his gaze. It worried her almost as much as the inexplicable behaviour of the palace guards.

The man's eyes were blue-grey. Light-coloured eyes

weren't uncommon in Jeirut's provinces, crossed by ancient trade routes between Europe, Asia and Africa. Yet Ghizlan had never seen eyes like this. Even as she watched the hint of blue was erased and his eyes under straight black eyebrows turned cool as mountain mist.

He had a wide forehead, a strong nose a little askew from an old break and a mouth that flattened disapprovingly.

Ghizlan arched her eyebrows. Whoever he was, he knew nothing about common courtesy, much less court etiquette. It was not for him to approve or disapprove.

Especially when he looked like he'd stalked in from the stables with his shaggy black hair curling around his collar and his jaw dark with several days' growth. It wasn't carefully sculpted designer stubble on that squared-off jaw but the beard of a man who simply hadn't bothered to shave for a week.

He stepped closer and she caught a whiff of horse and tangy male sweat. It was a strangely appealing smell, not sour but altogether intriguing.

'That's hardly a friendly greeting, Your Highness.' His words were soft but so resonant they eddied through her insides in the most unsettling way.

'It wasn't meant as a greeting. And I prefer not to be addressed as Highness.' She might be of royal blood but she'd never be ruler. Despite the modernisation of Jeirut, of which her father had been so proud, there was no question of equality of the sexes extending that far.

The intruder didn't make a move, either to remove his weapon or himself. Instead he angled his head to one side as if taking her measure. His eyes never left hers and heat sparked at the intensity of that look.

Who was this man who entered without a knock and didn't bother to introduce himself?

'Please remove your weapon while you're here.'

One dark eyebrow rose as if he'd never heard such a request. Silently he crossed his arms over his chest.

Make me.

He might as well have said it out loud. The challenge sizzled in the air between them.

Bizarrely, instead of being scared by this big, bold, *armed* brute, Ghizlan's blood fizzed as if trading glares with him had finally woken her from the curious, dormant feeling that had encompassed her since the news of her father's death.

She kept her hands relaxed at her sides but allowed her mouth to quirk up in the tiniest show of superiority. 'Your manners as much as your appearance make it clear you're a stranger to the palace and the niceties of polite society.'

His eyes narrowed and Ghizlan felt that stare as if it penetrated her silk-lined suit to graze her flesh.

Then in one swift movement he hauled his dagger from his belt and threw it.

Ghizlan's breath stopped in her throat and she knew her eyes widened but she didn't flinch when the unsheathed blade skidded across the desk an arm's length away.

Slowly she turned her head, seeing the jagged cut in the polished wood. Her father had prized that desk, not for its monetary value, but for the fact it had belonged to an ancestor who had introduced Jeirut's first constitution. A visionary, her father had called him. His role model.

Ghizlan stared at the deep, haphazard scratch on the beautiful wood and anger welled, raw and potent. An anger born of shock and loss. She knew the stranger's aim was deliberate. If he'd planned to attack her he wouldn't have missed.

Why inflict such wanton damage except to make a point of his rudeness? And, of course, to frighten her. Yet it wasn't fear bubbling up inside her. It was wrath.

Her father had devoted his life, and hers, to the betterment of their people. He may not have been a loving father but he deserved greater respect in death.

She made no move to grab the weapon. She was fit but no match for the sheer bulk of the man filling her father's study with his presence. He could probably snap her wrist with a single hand and no doubt he'd enjoy demonstrating his greater physical strength like a typical bully. But she refused to be cowed. She swung to face him.

'Barbarian.'

He didn't even blink. 'And you're a pampered waste of space. But let's not allow name-calling to get in the way of a sensible conversation.'

Ghizlan almost wished she *had* lunged for the knife. She wasn't accustomed to such rudeness and for the first time ever her blood surged with the desire to hurt someone. Slapping him would probably only bruise her palm when it came into contact with that high, sharp cheekbone. But with a knife…

She dragged in a fortifying breath and squashed the errant bloodlust. She blamed it on the creeping certainty that something terrible had happened here. Something that brought unfamiliar faces and armed guards to the royal palace that had epitomised the peace her father had worked so hard to win.

Mina! Where was her sister? Was she safe?

Fear skittered through her but Ghizlan wouldn't let it show. She wouldn't reveal it to the man looking so predatory. His eyes never wavered from her face as if he searched for weakness.

Ignoring the tremor in her knees, Ghizlan crossed the fine silk carpet and pulled out her father's chair from the desk. Deliberately she sank onto the padded leather and planted her arms on the chair, for all the world as if she belonged in her father's place.

If she was going to face this lout she'd do it from the position of power.

Too late she realised that while he stood, dominating the space with his size and raw energy, she was forced to tilt her neck to view him.

'Who are you?' She was relieved to hear her voice revealed none of the emotions roiling inside.

An instant longer that clear, cold gaze rested on her, then he bowed, surprisingly gracefully. It made her wonder what he did when he wasn't trespassing and threatening unarmed women. There was a magnetism about him that would make him unforgettable even if he hadn't barged, uninvited into this inner sanctum.

'I am Huseyn al Rasheed. I come from Jumeah.'

Huseyn al Rasheed. Ghizlan's stomach plunged and her brow puckered before she smoothed it into an expression of calm.

Trouble. That was who he was. Trouble with a capital T.

'The Iron Hand of Jumeah.' Fear prickled her nape.

'Some call me that.'

Ghizlan sucked in a surreptitious breath between her teeth. This grew worse and worse.

'Who can blame them? You have a reputation for destruction and brute force.'

She paused, marshalling her thoughts. Huseyn al Rasheed was son to the Sheikh of Jumeah, leader of the furthest province from the capital. Though part of Jeirut it was semi-autonomous and had a reputation for fearsome warriors.

Huseyn al Rasheed was notorious as his father's enforcer in the continuous border skirmishes with their nation's most difficult neighbour, Halarq. It had been her father's dearest hope that the peace treaties he'd been negotiating with both Halarq and their other neighbouring nation, Zahrat, would end generations of unrest. Unrest Huseyn al Rasheed and his father only fed with their confrontational behaviour.

Ghizlan gripped the leather armrests tight, wishing

her father were here to deal with this. 'Did your father send you?'

'No one sent me. My father, like his cousin, *your* father, is dead.'

Second cousin, Ghizlan almost blurted, wanting to deny the connection he claimed, but she was well trained in holding her tongue.

'My condolences on your loss.' Though she saw nothing in that tough, determined face remotely resembling grief.

'And my condolences on yours.'

Ghizlan nodded, the movement jerky. She didn't like the way he stared at her. Like a big cat who'd found some fascinating new prey to torment.

She curled her fingers until her nails dug into leather. This was no time for flights of fantasy.

'And your reason for entering here, armed and uninvited?'

Was it imagination again or did something flicker in those grey eyes? Surely not because she'd called him on his deplorable behaviour? If the rumours surrounding this man were true she needed to tread very, very carefully.

'I'm here to claim the crown of Jeirut.'

Ghizlan's heart stopped then sprinted on frantically.

'By force of arms?' Vaguely Ghizlan wondered at her ability to sound calm when horror was turning her very bones cold. A man like the Iron Hand in control of her beloved country? They'd be at war in a week. All her father's work, and her own, undone.

Pain lanced her chest and her lungs cramped. She blinked and forced herself to breathe.

'I have no intention of starting a civil war.'

'Which doesn't answer my question.'

He shrugged and Ghizlan watched, mesmerised, as those impossibly broad shoulders lifted.

Terror, loathing, anger. That's what she should feel. Yet

that tingling sensation across her breasts and down to her belly didn't seem like any of those.

She ignored it. She was stressed and anxious.

'I have no intention of fighting my own people for the royal sheikhdom.'

The constriction banding her chest eased a little. Yet she didn't trust this man. Everything about him set alarm bells ringing.

'You think the elders will vote for a man like *you* as leader?' She couldn't sit still. She surged to her feet, her hands clenched in fists on the desk as she leaned forward. How dared he walk in here as if he owned the place?

'I'm sure they'll see the wisdom of choosing me.' He paused, long enough for a flicker of heat to pass between them. Banked fury, Ghizlan decided. 'Especially given the other happy circumstance.'

'Happy circumstance?' Ghizlan frowned.

'My wedding.'

Ghizlan opened her mouth but realised she would only parrot what he had said. Instead she stood, tension racking her body as she watched his mouth curve up in a smile that was painfully smug. It transformed his face enough that she wondered how he'd look if something genuinely amused him. Heat drilled through her. She could almost see traces of a handsome man beneath that fierce beard and the threat he represented. Then she reminded herself this man didn't do light-hearted. And even if he did she wasn't interested in seeing it.

'That's my other reason for coming to the capital. To claim my bride.'

Ghizlan loathed his superior, über-confident air, the gloating note in his deep voice.

She pitied his bride, whoever she was, but clearly he wanted her to be impressed. What would it cost her to play along at least until she got to the bottom of this?

'Who are you marrying? Do I know her?'

His smile widened and she saw the gleam of strong white teeth. Fear scudded down her spine as she read his expression.

'That would be you, my dear Ghizlan. I'm taking you as my wife.'

CHAPTER TWO

HER EYES WIDENED and Huseyn's satisfaction splintered. He'd expected shock, but not the absolute horror he read on her face.

He was a rough and ready soldier but he wasn't a monster. Her expression made him feel like he'd threatened to molest her, instead of honourably planning to marry her.

It was his own fault. He hadn't meant to spring it on her like that. But the high and mighty Princess provoked him as no one had succeeded in doing.

He should have expected the unexpected. Selim had warned before he entered the room that she wasn't what they'd thought. She had grit. She'd even scolded Selim, his right-hand man, now captain of the royal guard, about his lack of courtesy and defied him despite the guards surrounding her!

Huseyn would love to have seen that.

But now he had his hands full with a woman who flouted his assumptions.

Steadfastly he refused to let his gaze flick down over her ripe, enticing body. Yet it was too late because the memory of it taunted, threatening to distract him.

He'd entered the room to find her braced over the desk. He'd had a perfect view of shapely legs and a trim, beautifully rounded backside in that tight skirt. When she'd straightened and tugged at her clothes, wriggling her hips as she did, flame had seared him. Then she'd turned and faced him down as if he were something slimy on the sole of her high-heeled shoe.

No man would dare look at him that way. As for

women—he was used to them sighing over his muscles and his stamina.

When the Princess raised those perfect eyebrows at him all he'd felt was heat.

And curiosity.

'That's totally absurd! I'm not your dear. And I didn't give you permission to call me Ghizlan.'

Anger emphasised her beauty, bringing colour to those slanted cheekbones, making her eyes sparkle and her whole being vibrate with energy. He'd known from the photos that she was lovely, but those images of her at royal events, lips curved in a polite smile, didn't do her justice.

He'd underestimated her. The way she'd stood up to him, not flinching when he'd thrown his knife, had made him rethink. She'd defied him even though she must know she'd been outmanoeuvred. Huseyn admired her for that.

'What am I to call you if not Ghizlan?' His voice dropped on her name as he savoured the taste of it. What would *she* taste like? Sugary sweet or spicy hot like those burning, dark eyes?

He'd considered her a tool to be exploited and a necessary encumbrance. He hadn't expected to desire her.

That was one thing in her favour. She was a woman of passion, despite how she strove to hide it. And a woman of experience, that went without saying. At twenty-six, and after living abroad in the US and Sweden, she was no shrinking maiden. His belly tightened in anticipation. He didn't particularly want to marry but since it was necessary, he'd prefer a wife who could satisfy his physical needs.

'*My lady* is the correct form of address.'

Huseyn stared at her chiselled features, her head held high as if wearing a crown. As if looking down on a man who'd toiled all his life in service to his Sheikh and his people. This from a woman who'd never done a day's work in her life. Who'd never held down a job or done anything but live off the nation's largesse.

Deliberately Huseyn let his gaze slide down her hourglass figure, lingering on the swell of her breasts, the narrowness of her waist, then the lush curve of hips and thighs. When his gaze rose her face was pink but her expression gave nothing away, except for her flattened lips.

She didn't like him looking at her.

She should be grateful he only looked. The way she'd met him challenge for challenge, refusing to be bested, was an enticing invitation. So was the heavy throb of awareness clogging the air. They might be enemies but he sensed there were things they would both enjoy together.

'Does the title make you feel superior to a mere soldier? Even though it was awarded because of an accident of birth?'

Huseyn had met many who'd fancied themselves better than him. He was illegitimate and his mother had been poor and uneducated, despite the looks that had captured his father's eye. But it had been a long time since anyone had dared look down on him. Not since he'd grown old enough to fight and prove himself as a warrior of strength and honour.

'I believe in common courtesy.' Her gaze met his unflinchingly and, to his astonishment, Huseyn felt a niggle of…could it be shame?

'As you point out, my title is honorary.' She stood straighter, lifting her fists from the table and looking down her regal nose at him in a way that, perversely, made him want to applaud. How many women in her position would stand resolute? 'Some would say I've spent a lifetime living up to the title but I'm sure you—' she sent him a smile as cool as cut glass '—aren't interested in that.' She paused for just a beat. 'What should I call you?'

'Huseyn will do.' He was Sheikh of his province but soon he would rule the nation and Ghizlan would be his wife. Even if the marriage was for political reasons, he discovered he wanted to hear his name on her lips.

His brain stalled on an unexpected vision of her naked beneath him, her soft body welcoming, her breathing ragged as she clutched him, crying out his name in ecstasy.

He couldn't remember such instantaneous, all-consuming lust. It must be the result of months too busy even to take a night off to be with a woman.

'Well, Huseyn.' Her voice crackled with ice but strangely he enjoyed even that. 'Whatever your plans, marrying me isn't possible.'

'Why?' He folded his arms and watched her gaze sharpen. In any other woman he'd have put that fleeting expression down to feminine interest. Yet Ghizlan could be masking fear. He needed to remember that. 'You're available since the Sheikh of Zahrat jilted you.'

It had been the scandal of the decade and the sort of snub to Jeirut that Huseyn would not allow once he ruled. It was time the neighbouring nations paid Jeirut respect.

Ghizlan mirrored him, crossing her arms, and for a second he was distracted by the rising swell of her breasts and the shadow of her cleavage.

This woman fought with weapons more dangerous than guns or knives.

'I was not jilted,' she said coolly. 'I met Sheikh Idris as part of my father's push for a trade and peace deal with Zahrat. As for us marrying...' She shook her head. 'I was happy to attend his betrothal ceremony in London.'

'But not his recent wedding.' Huseyn surveyed her keenly, interested, despite himself, in her feelings for the man who'd dumped her when he'd discovered he had a son by an Englishwoman he hadn't seen in years. A woman he'd since married.

'It wasn't possible. I had business commitments elsewhere.'

It wasn't a convincing lie but he gave her marks for trying. What *had* she felt for Idris? The idea of her nursing a broken heart was vaguely...unsettling.

'Business?'

'Strange as it may seem to you—' her eyes flicked from him dismissively '—I do have some business interests.'

That was news but Huseyn didn't show it.

'And you're free to marry.'

Fine eyebrows arched in a haughty show of surprise that made him long to wrap his hand around that slender neck and draw her close enough to kiss. Her touch-me-not air was a surprising turnon. He couldn't understand it. His taste had never run to spoiled rich girls.

'I have no plans to.'

'No need. I've made the plans already.'

'But—'

'Or did I get it wrong? Aren't you up for sale? Willing to go to the highest bidder? Weren't you part of the price your father planned to pay for a treaty with Zahrat?'

Her face remained as unruffled as ever but something flashed across her eyes that made him think he'd hurt her. Yet how could that be? She'd been bred to be a dynastic bargaining chip.

'Contrary to the old-fashioned customs in your province, Huseyn—' his name on her lips was a silky taunt '—I'm not a chattel. Thanks to my father, women have a say in their lives here now. I have a will of my own.'

He saw that, and despite the minor inconvenience of dealing with it, Huseyn was glad. He admired spirit. If he was to be shackled to her, at least it would be interesting, once she stopped defying him and accepted the inevitable.

'You're afraid I can't meet your bride price?'

'I'm not interested in how many camels you offer for my hand.' As if he were a poor herder from a backward province. 'And I'm not afraid. I'm not afraid of any man.' She drew herself even taller, betraying the anxiety she tried to conceal. Reading opponents' body language could save your life in combat. Huseyn had learned that early.

'I won't hurt you, Ghizlan.' He should have said it

sooner, but he'd been too caught up sparring with her, enjoying the cut and thrust of parrying her objections.

Reassuring women didn't come naturally. He led warriors and protected his people. He knew a lot about women, in bed at least, but he wasn't used to negotiating with them. His was a man's world.

She blinked and for a second he thought he glimpsed a vulnerable woman behind the calm façade. Then she was gone, replaced by an arrogant aristocrat.

'And my sister? Have you hurt her?'

'Of course not!' His pride pricked. She really did think him uncivilised. 'Princess Mina is in her rooms.'

If he expected to win thanks from Her Royal Haughtiness he was doomed to disappointment. Her eyes snapped to his as she did her best to cut him down with that cool stare. Yet all he felt was a jolt of sexual awareness. And a sliver of anticipation at the idea of taming this disdainful Princess.

'Thank you for the assurance.' Her tone was lofty. 'I appreciate it given the illegal presence of armed men in the palace.'

Huseyn frowned. He understood she'd had a fright but surely even here his reputation for protecting the weak, including women, was known. His might be a pre-emptive strike to secure the throne but they weren't criminals. He had a legitimate claim to rule. The *best* claim.

'The guards are here for protection.'

Again that supercilious lift of dark eyebrows. 'And the palace guards who were here before?'

'Temporarily relieved of duty.'

'If you've hurt any of them—'

'No one has been hurt.' Except the soldier who'd tried to quieten the younger Princess, Mina, and been bitten on the hand. Huseyn should have realised then that these spoiled women would be trouble. 'There has been no fighting.'

It hadn't been necessary. Huseyn had visited the palace

to pay his respects to his late King. Once inside, and with the Princess Mina a hostage to their good behaviour, it had been easy to convince the palace guard to stand down.

'Good, then you won't object to me seeing the Captain of the Guard. The *real* one.' When he remained silent she tilted her head and assessed him. 'Unless you're frightened to allow me that courtesy.'

This woman knew how to get under his skin. He, the Iron Hand of Jumeah, frightened! No man would dare even think it.

Ghizlan's breath rushed out in a shaky sigh. Talking to this man was like addressing a brick wall. Except for the curious spark of awareness when his gaze moved over her.

She should be petrified. She *was* anxious, particularly for Mina, but at the same time she felt more energised than she had in ages.

Her lips flattened as she tried to suppress gallows humour. Nothing like an armed coup and the threat of imprisonment to shake you up!

'What's wrong?' His broad brow furrowed and, if she didn't know better, she'd almost think he looked concerned.

The idea was beyond laughable.

He was a brute. An opportunist who sought to profit from her father's death.

He saw her as a chattel.

Like your father did.

The memory stabbed. Huseyn was right. Her father had viewed her and Mina as assets to further his plans. Marrying her to a neighbouring sheikh had been part of his negotiations. It had hurt when her father told her, even though she'd been raised to expect an arranged marriage.

For years she'd been obedient, dutiful, putting her country's needs first. Yet not once had that gained her a father's love or appreciation. He'd relied on her as a matter of course, never considering her happiness.

She'd be damned if she'd have this…interloper tell her who she could marry! She might be bound to her country by ties of duty and love, but for the first time she was free to live as she chose. She did *not* choose to tie herself to an uncivilised bully.

Ghizlan stalked around the desk so she stood before Huseyn al Rasheed, tilting her chin to glare into his pale eyes. The evocative scent of warm, male skin filtered into her senses. She ignored it, as she ignored the fact that up close there was absolutely no doubt he was boldly attractive, despite the beard and rumpled hair and arrogance.

'You ask me what's wrong?' She laughed, the sound brittle. 'What could possibly be wrong? Apart from the fact you've taken over the palace in some sort of revolution and demand I marry you. You deny me access to my sister. You won't let me see the staff. How do I know they're all right?'

'Because you have my word. And I haven't denied you access to your sister.'

'I can see her?' She hadn't pressed because she feared most for their staff. Mina's royal position gave her some protection, but the people who worked in the palace had no one but her to fight for them.

Relief was so strong it was a punch to the belly. Ghizlan locked her knees to stop herself swaying. She refused to show weakness.

'You can see her when we finish our discussion.'

'Is that what you call it?'

His mouth twisted and she wondered if it was in anger or frustration. She didn't care. She was dangerously close to losing her cool. She'd fought to keep her composure, knowing it was the only way to make him take her, and her demands for the people relying on her, seriously. But she didn't know how long she could keep this up.

'Of course.' He unfolded his arms and abruptly she was aware of how close they stood, and how very big he was.

Heat emanated from him, warming her despite the chill gripping her bones. It was an insidious warmth, like the strange flutter of awareness rippling through her when his broad shoulders lifted then settled again.

She'd never been close to a man so blatantly *masculine*. Not just in size and brute strength, but with a potent, unfamiliar *something* that made her body want to shiver and melt at the same time.

'I'll see the Captain of the Guard first. I need to check the staff are all right.' She paused as fear for her personal bodyguard struck. She hadn't seen them since the plane. 'And my bodyguard. I need to make sure—'

He raised one big hand, palm out. 'They're unharmed.'

'You'll forgive me for needing to see proof for myself.' She paused, fighting fear that those who'd devoted themselves to protecting her family had been harmed. 'Then I'll see my sister.'

Ghizlan made to walk away but his long arm snapped out and strong fingers shackled her wrist.

Her pulse thudded, staccato and strong. She hated that he could feel it with his bare hand on her wrist. She particularly hated the effervescence that radiated through her from his touch.

'I prefer not to be manhandled.'

'Manhandled?' A jet eyebrow rose and the lips buried in all that undergrowth of beard curved up.

She amused him. The realisation infuriated her.

'I'm not a plaything, Huseyn. You'll find most women prefer not to be touched against their will.'

'Most women enjoy my touch.' His voice was a low murmur of masculine confidence. His eyes gleamed silver. He thought himself irresistible.

The women in his province of Jumeah must be a sorry lot.

Impossible, appalling man. Was she supposed to thank him for planning to marry her?

'If you say so.' She met his look blandly. 'But I can't help thinking most women would *pretend* to enjoy intimacy when a man has so much more...power than they do. Out of self-defence, you understand.'

He dropped her hand as if bitten, his eyes widening in what looked like genuine shock.

'I would never use force against a woman!' His growl scuttled along her spine, drawing her skin tight.

'Is that so?' She stepped back until she felt the desk behind her. It was good to lean on something solid. 'Then what would you call your demand that we marry? If it's a request, I've already declined.'

Ghizlan saw his jaw move. Was he grinding his teeth? She hoped he got jaw ache. A pulse throbbed at his temple and the muscles in those big arms bunched and swelled.

She refused to cower.

Always show a calm face, no matter what the provocation.

'It's an attempt to avoid bloodshed.'

'You'll have to do better than that. Jeirut is a proud and stable democratic monarchy. The new Sheikh will be voted in by the Royal Council, then parliament. There will be no bloodshed. The truth is you want the crown and you're resorting to force to get it.'

'Not force. Just a pre-emptive tactical move.'

Ghizlan remained scornfully silent.

He scowled at her and she knew she should be scared. But to her surprise, she was more intrigued than fearful. Clearly she was jet-lagged and had taken leave of her senses!

'Even you must admit I'm the best choice to rule. I have a solid claim to the crown with my kinship ties. I'm the only one who can say that. More importantly, I'm strong, resolute, a warrior as well as having experience as an administrator. Our marriage will simply make the decision easier and speed the process.'

Ghizlan arched one eyebrow. 'If you're such a perfect choice the Council will vote for you.'

'But that will take *time*. Time Jeirut doesn't have.'

'You may be eager to ascend the throne but—'

'You think this is about *me*?' His shaggy hair brushed his shirt as he shook his head. 'It's about keeping Jeirut safe. With your father's death, Halarq is poised to invade.'

'Nonsense.' Her voice sharpened. 'My father was on the brink of signing peace agreements with both Zahrat and Halarq.'

'Now he's gone the old Emir of Halarq sees an opportunity. His troops are mobilising. Intelligence suggests they'll begin by claiming the disputed territory then pushing as far as they can into Jeirut.'

'That territory has belonged to Jeirut for two hundred years.'

'Yet I've been fighting border skirmishes with his forces since I was old enough to hold a weapon. You may not realise it here in the safety of the capital.' His gaze raked the room as if dismissing its fine furnishings. 'But my province has borne the brunt of our neighbour's ambitions for years. Believe me, he's poised to act and the longer it takes us to choose a new leader the better it suits him.'

Ghizlan opened her mouth to protest then closed it. There was a seed of truth in what Huseyn said. 'Then talk to the Council. Urge a speedy decision.'

He shook his head. 'The majority are in favour of me but the Council likes to deliberate. A quick decision is seen as a bad one. And there are two other candidates, though their claims aren't as strong. If Halarq invades it will throw that process into confusion. I need to act now. Convince the Council to choose the best man to protect the country.'

Ghizlan looked at the determined thrust of that dark jaw, and the gleam in his eyes, and she nearly believed him. Until she thought of her sister and the palace in lockdown.

Her hands came together in slow, deliberate applause.

'That's some performance. I could almost believe you were sacrificing yourself for the country in claiming the throne. But if you expect me to sacrifice *my* liberty and marry you, think again. Your rhetoric doesn't sway me.'

Something flickered across his face. An expression so swift she couldn't read it. Yet it reminded her of a flash of sheet lightning across mountain peaks in the storm season. Her flesh tightened.

'You won't do this for your country?'

'For my country or for you?' She didn't bother hiding her disdain.

He scowled. 'I should have known not to expect too much from you. You didn't even hurry home when your father died. Obviously your priorities lie elsewhere.'

Ghizlan sucked in an outraged breath. It was true she'd avoided returning to Jeirut when her planned betrothal to Sheikh Idris was abruptly cancelled. But that had been at her father's request, to let the scandal die. Since then she'd been cultivating business contacts Jeirut desperately needed if planned new developments were to proceed.

Not that a man like this, a ruthless mountain marauder with no finesse, would understand that.

'Clearly news is slow to reach your province,' she bit out. 'The dust cloud from a volcano in Iceland stopped all flights for days.' She'd almost flown home from New York across the Pacific instead but each day the forecasters had predicted the cloud would clear and aviation would recommence. For two days they'd been wrong. 'I came on the first flight.'

Her voice grew husky. It was ridiculous. She'd never been close to her father. He'd never once indicated he loved her. Yet her chest ached when she thought of not being here for his funeral. Or to support Mina.

'Not that I care about your opinion. I'd simply never marry a man I despised on sight.'

'Despised?' His voice dropped to that bass rumble.

Thunder to the lightning she'd seen a moment ago. She felt its vibration shimmer across her nipples and thighs.

'Absolutely.' Her chin notched even higher. Had he moved closer?

He *had* moved closer. She drew in that tangy scent of stable and man as he stepped in, toe to toe.

'Then how do you explain *this*, my lady?'

Big, warm, implacable hands closed around her upper arms and his face lowered to hers.

CHAPTER THREE

GHIZLAN WHIPPED HER head to one side but only succeeded in baring her cheek to this…this…bandit.

Whiskers brushed her in a totally unfamiliar caress, sending little shivers dancing across her skin. Warm lips, far softer than she'd imagined, nuzzled her cheek, stealing her breath.

She wouldn't scream. She wouldn't give him the pleasure of revealing fear. Instead she stood ramrod straight. Frozen.

Yet it wasn't fear she experienced as his lips moved in a tantalisingly slow trail up to her ear. Ghizlan blinked, surprised at the odd sensation of warmth curling in on itself deep in her belly.

This had gone on long enough.

She yanked her arms back, trying to break his hold, but it was like wrestling a boulder. A huge, warm boulder scented not just with the stables but with an enticing, unfamiliar tang that she suspected was essence of Huseyn al Rasheed.

Teeth nipped her earlobe and she jumped, horrified at the fiery trail zapping from the spot straight to her womb, as if he'd jerked a string and she, like a puppet, responded. Her nipples budded hard and achy against her bra. Did he feel that as his big body pressed against her?

'Stop it, you lout!'

Hands braced on his chest, she leaned back, trying to escape, but he was taller and stronger. In one swift movement he clamped both her hands against that brawny, powerful chest. His other hand grabbed the back of her head, inexorably turning her face towards him.

Ghizlan saw a flash of smoky blue beneath straight dark brows, then his mouth was on hers.

Heat, power, the rich, zesty scent of male skin. The soft prickle of his whiskers against her flesh contrasted with the sheer force of his mouth grinding down on hers. It was a predictably ruthless assault on her senses by a man determined to dominate.

Fear filtered into her stunned brain. Until she realised, astonished, that despite the power in that massive, muscled body, he'd pulled back a fraction. Even as the thought formed, the pressure on her lips eased and his hand in her hair gentled, cradling and massaging.

Ghizlan stared, trying to focus on the blue of his eyes, but he was too close. He shifted his stance, drawing her lower body in against him until there was no mistaking the monumental evidence of his arousal.

She gasped, stunned, and too late realised her mistake. For Huseyn al Rasheed took the opportunity to invade her mouth.

Not to ravage this time but to seduce. His movements were sure but gentle as his tongue swiped hers, learning the feel and taste of her, just as she discovered he tasted like almonds and something else impossibly, horrifyingly delicious.

Her chest cramped as she realised she *enjoyed* the sensation of his tongue tangling with hers.

Foggily she fought the drugging pleasure of those slow, sure, sensual movements of lips and tongue, no longer forcing but *inviting*.

A shiver passed from the back of her skull where his fingers caressed her, down to her curling toes.

She'd been kissed before. Perfectly pleasant kisses from perfectly nice men. Sweet kisses, even eager kisses. But none like this. None that *demanded* so imperiously then gentled to seduce her into feelings that surely were more dangerous than anything else he could unleash on her.

His kiss invited her to relax and follow the unfamiliar lure of pleasure. To be selfish, just once. His hand cupping her head supported but also caressed, sending whorls of languid delight through her.

And his hard body against hers—*that* was a totally new, electrifying experience. Ghizlan had kissed, and dated while a student, but, ever conscious of the high expectations placed on her, and the possibility for scandal if caught out publicly in a love affair, she'd never progressed beyond that.

No man had ever made her feel this potent longing for more.

Ghizlan tried to be strong, tried not to respond. Until she heard, and tasted, Huseyn's low humming growl of satisfaction. It was a sensual assault, as real as his hand in her hair or his tongue stroking hers. The way it vibrated through her, sparking an answering excitement, was unlike anything she'd known.

His kiss slowed, deepened, became positively languorous, and Ghizlan's bones began to soften. Her hands twitched against that powerful chest and before she knew it they'd slid up, over hard shoulders to tangle in tousled locks, tunnelling and tugging then clamping tight on his skull.

She shifted, angling her mouth to kiss him back and losing her breath as his erection aligned provocatively against her.

Another growl from the back of his throat and he roped one muscled arm around her, lifting her against him so the contact became even more blatantly sexual.

And devastatingly delicious.

Ghizlan gasped, her mind, like her body, running on overdrive. One part of her was aware of curving in, inviting more of that heavy, outrageously improper contact. Another revelled in the strength of a man who could lift her with one arm as if she were made of gossamer. But mainly she was focused on the provocative, delicious kiss she didn't want to end.

Except this was wrong. On so many levels she couldn't begin to count them.

The part of her consciousness that had been trained from birth to focus on duty, to be a good example, to do the right thing always, suddenly burst awake and screamed in horror.

Ghizlan dropped her hands to his shoulders and shoved with all her might. She tried to tear her mouth away and only succeeded in inviting him to nuzzle her neck.

Her body trembled and flushed with delight at the sensations bombarding her from his mouth and his hands and that huge body moving deliberately against her pelvis.

'I don't want this. Do you hear me? I don't want it!' Her voice was a raw whiplash, ragged and desperate. 'Let me go.' She gave up pushing and thumped her fists on his shoulders.

Finally, slowly, his head lifted. His eyes pinioned her as effectively as that heavy arm lashing her to him. His gaze was the colour of the sky after sunset, that fleeting blue when the first stars appeared before the sky turned indigo.

He blinked. Once. Twice. His gaze dropped to her lips, throbbing and heavy from that devastating kiss. To Ghizlan's horror she felt that stare like a stroking caress.

'Let me go.' This time her voice was subdued. How she managed to look him in the eye, Ghizlan couldn't fathom. They both knew that despite her anger she'd responded, lost to everything but the magic of his kiss.

Heat roared in her veins. Shame filled her that she should surrender so easily to such a man!

She told herself she'd responded because of her inexperience. If she'd known what to expect she could have prepared herself. She'd known he fancied himself as a lover—that smugness had been unmistakable. Clearly he'd played his greater expertise to advantage.

'Well, that was interesting.' His voice held a husky note that drove a shaft of heat right to her belly.

'You can let me go now.'

His lips curved slowly into a smile Ghizlan wanted to hate because it was prompted by masculine pride. He was pleased with himself because she hadn't been able to resist him. But strangely his smile made her heart thud faster.

'Are you sure you can stand?'

Of all the complacent, self-satisfied...

Ghizlan's knee-jerk reaction, straight for the soft spot where that monumental male ego was centred, should have crippled him. But his reactions were faster than hers. Her knee grazed his cotton trousers but he'd already whipped back out of reach with the lightning reflexes of a man used to fighting. And fighting dirty.

His hands dropped, leaving her free, panting for breath and propped against the desk.

At least that wiped the grin off his insufferable face.

Ghizlan summoned her strength, standing tall, her hands going automatically to her hair and swiftly pinning what he'd turned into a mare's nest. Fortunately she could tidy her hair without thinking about it, like she could descend a grand staircase in a full-length dress without looking down or tripping. Or converse with ambassadors in several languages at the same time. Years of practice made some things easy.

What she found difficult was the realisation her own body had betrayed her.

'You've had your fun at my expense.' She kept her voice even, only because letting him glimpse the depth of her despair at her weakness was untenable. 'Now, I'd like the see the Captain of the Guard, and my bodyguards and then my sister.'

'After we've concluded our business.'

Ghizlan shook her head. 'That can wait.' She hefted a breath, waiting for some tiny sign he relented but none came. He remained immovable, implacable.

She sighed and fought the desire to rub her aching head. 'Surely you understand I must see them. They're my responsibility. With my father…gone, it's my duty to see to their welfare.' She swallowed, hating the salty tangle of tiredness and emotion blocking her throat. She couldn't afford to be weak now. 'You'd feel the same way about the soldiers you command.'

He'd give her points for perceptiveness. Ghizlan understood him better than he'd expected. Appealing to his sense of duty to his men was the approach he'd expect of an honourable adversary, a general he could respect, even if they were on opposite sides.

He hadn't thought a pretty princess, spoiled from birth and raised in luxury, would understand that overriding sense of responsibility. Much less share it!

His gaze raked her. This time he tried to take in more than the mutinous, deliciously kiss-swollen mouth, the delectable figure, flawless skin and glossy ebony hair that had run like silk in his hands.

Huseyn discovered an unwavering dark gaze, shoulders as straight as any guard on patrol, and an expression as cool as the snow on the topmost peaks of Jeirut's highest mountain range. Only the throbbing pulse hammering at her throat belied her calm façade. It ignited a flare of satisfaction that he'd got to her as she had him.

Admiration vied with impatience and lust. He wanted her mouth beneath his, eager and generous, that bountiful body crushed against his still painfully hard arousal.

He shook his head, appalled. This was no time to indulge himself. The future of his province and his country hung in the balance.

'What do you want? For me to beg? Is that what it will take to satisfy you?'

'You'd do that?' Huseyn imagined her on her knees before him, head bent. But the vision swimming before his eyes didn't involve her begging. With a roaring rush of arousal he realised it was something more satisfying, more earthy, that he desired from this proud princess.

She opened those reddened lips, now devoid of lipstick, and abruptly Huseyn had had enough. He'd have her in his bed soon enough, as his wife. Because he must and because he'd do what was necessary to make that happen. In the meantime he refused to toy with her. Her instincts were honourable and he respected that.

'No.' His voice was harsh. 'No, I don't expect you to beg.' He sucked air into constricted lungs and watched as her attention dropped to the rise of his chest, her eyes rounding infinitesimally. As if she liked what she saw.

She'd certainly enjoyed that kiss. She'd been so enthusiastic he'd actually begun to forget why he'd kissed her. To show who had the upper hand, and more, to puncture that haughty air of hers.

Realisation slammed into Huseyn and with it distaste. He'd let her distract him from his purpose. From the vital work that needed to be done.

'Wait here. I'll have them each brought to you so you can satisfy yourself that they're unharmed.'

'It would be easier if I went—'

'No.' A slashing gesture stopped her mid-sentence. There was no way he'd allow her to wander the palace. Not till everything was settled. 'Give me your phone and I'll arrange for them to see you here.'

'My phone?' She looked puzzled.

Huseyn folded his arms over his chest. 'I don't want you contacting people outside the palace till we've concluded our business.' Her gaze sliced to the phone on the desk.

He shook his head. 'The landlines have been temporarily disconnected. All electronic devices have been confiscated.'

'While you stage your coup.'

For a minute, caught up in appreciation of her bravery,

he'd almost forgotten his dislike of the pampered elite who sucked the country dry with their demands.

'While I save the nation.'

Her snort of derision was anything but regal and Huseyn found himself suppressing a smile. Despite everything, he warmed to this blue-blooded daughter of privilege.

She swung round, treating Huseyn to a view of her peach-perfect bottom as she leaned over to grab her purse.

'Here.' She extended her phone. 'But I expect it back intact. I'm in the middle of important negotiations and I want my contacts and messages untouched.'

Negotiations? With her hairstylist? Boyfriends? Huseyn didn't care. She'd be incommunicado till he said so.

His fingers closed around the phone, his big hand scraping her smaller one, and heat shot up his arm. He frowned, lips flattening at that unwanted response.

She pulled her hand back, her face smoothing into the mask of calm he'd learned she wore when something disturbed her. Good. He liked the idea that he disturbed her. For she sure as hell disturbed him!

'The phone will be returned undamaged.' He paused. 'As long as you obey orders.'

Ebony eyebrows arched but she said nothing. She was learning.

'After you've assured yourself no one has been harmed, we'll talk.' With that he turned and left. He had business to attend to. He'd deal with his recalcitrant bride later.

'Truly, I'm fine.' Mina squeezed Ghizlan's hand. 'But I'm glad you're here. It's been pretty grim.'

Ghizlan nodded, the banked embers of fury glowing brighter. Mina was just seventeen. Losing her father was bad enough without being held prisoner in her own home.

'You're sure they didn't hurt you? You'd tell me, wouldn't you?'

'Of course. But they didn't hurt me. Just took my phone

and laptop and told me I couldn't leave the palace.' Her mouth set in a distressed line. 'But I need to access the net, Ghizlan. It's vital.'

'Vital?' It was such a relief seeing her sister okay. First the Captain of the Palace Guard then her own protection staff. Now Mina. It seemed Huseyn al Rasheed was as good as his word. No one had been harmed. The takeover had been accomplished with the ease and precision of a consummate professional.

A professional coup leader, she reminded herself. And a thug. Look at the way he'd groped her.

'Are you listening, Ghizlan?'

'Of course.' She smiled. 'But I'm still getting used to your new look.'

Mina stroked the dark hair feathering her bare neck. 'When Father died I realised that at last I could do what I wanted. Not pretend to be someone I'm not.' Her expression grew earnest. 'I'm not like you, Ghizlan. I can't be the consummate diplomat, following duty and public expectation. I tried to please Father but never succeeded. As for studying economics...' She shuddered.

Ghizlan covered Mina's hand with hers, emotion welling. 'You're fine as you are, Mina. You're bright and enthusiastic and talented.' It seemed like betrayal to think it but with their father's death Mina was free to follow her inclinations and build the life she wanted. Their father couldn't straitjacket *her* into a life designed to fulfil some political objective as he had Ghizlan.

'Actually, I rebelled a while ago. Before Father died, though he didn't know.' Mina's eyes glowed. 'You know I don't want to go to that stuffy school to study economics.'

'I know.' It had been part of their father's plan to show Jeiruti women could achieve in nontraditional fields. Which was why Ghizlan had a degree in chemical engineering, though at least she'd been interested in science in the first place. 'So what have you done?'

'I applied to art school. A fabulous art school in France. You know that's always been my dream. I secretly sent off an application and offers should be out now but I can't check my email.' Her voice rose in distress. 'If they make an offer and I don't reply, they won't wait. They'll—'

'Calm down, Mina. They'll give you time to respond.'

'Not if we're in lockdown for weeks. What if Huseyn doesn't release us for months? What if—?'

'Don't fret. He can't hold us indefinitely. His plan is to get himself declared Sheikh as soon as possible.'

With her as a vital part of his plan. But he'd soon discover she was no gullible pawn. She'd never marry him.

'You really think so? I'd shrivel up and die if I had to do the course Father picked.'

'No one's going to force you to do anything, Mina. Just relax.'

The thought struck Ghizlan with the force of a lightning bolt. It was true. Once a new sheikh was proclaimed they would leave the palace. Huseyn couldn't force her to marry him. All she had to do was remain steadfast. When he'd given up they could do what they wanted with their lives. Mina could go to art school and she could... Her brow puckered. It had been so long since she'd thought about what *she* wanted, rather than what was expected, she didn't immediately know how she wanted to spend her future.

Now freedom beckoned. A whole world of opportunity.

'Ghizlan? You have the strangest look on your face.'

Ghizlan smiled. Not the polite smile she used for official occasions, but a beam of excitement. 'That's because I've realised once Huseyn al Rasheed gets what he wants we'll be free to do what *we* want. No one can stop us.'

'You demanded my presence?' Ghizlan lifted her chin to meet those misty blue eyes. The sheer size of the man would daunt her if she let it. She focused on that rather than the peculiar flutter of her pulse when his gaze met hers.

Antagonism. Distrust. That's what she felt.

The strange excitement she experienced when he turned from her father's desk to face her was due to the realisation she and Mina would soon be free in a way they'd never dreamed possible. It had nothing to do with the memory of Huseyn's lips on hers or that hollow ache in her middle when he'd crushed her to him. Or that, minus the long cloak, his pale trousers and shirt emphasised the breathtaking strength in that beautifully proportioned body.

Ghizlan preferred character to brawn.

'Gracious as ever, I see.' That deep voice was soft, like plush velvet across her skin. He didn't look annoyed either, merely watchful as she closed the study door and approached the desk.

That all-encompassing survey was incredibly disquieting. Ghizlan fought to repress a shiver.

'You expect me to pretend you and your thugs haven't invaded the capital or taken me and my sister hostage?' Ghizlan took a sustaining breath and was momentarily discomfited when his gaze flicked down as if taking stock of her body.

Rubbish. He wasn't interested in her. That scene he'd played out here a couple of hours earlier had been about power, not attraction. Some men got off on that. Men like Huseyn al Rasheed.

'You don't give up, do you?' He leaned back against her father's desk as if he owned it. The raw, jagged scratch he'd made in it was half hidden by papers. Ghizlan was incensed at how he'd made himself at home.

'You expect me to treat you like a welcome guest?'

'Frankly, my manners are the least of your worries, *my lady*. You should be more concerned about the threat to Jeirut from Halarq.'

'Ah, but according to you, I'm merely a waste of space.' She tilted her head as if thinking. As if she didn't recall precisely what he'd called her. 'A pampered princess, wasn't it? It's obvious that as far as you're concerned such weighty issues can only be dealt with by armed men. The sort of men who flout the law and imprison law-abiding citizens.'

Silver flashed in those deep-set eyes and he muttered something under his breath.

She locked her hands together behind her, forcing her shoulders back and her chin up. This was pointless. Much as she enjoyed baiting him, there was nothing to be gained from it except personal satisfaction. She had others in her care to worry about. She couldn't afford to endanger them.

'Might I suggest that, while the citadel is under armed guard, you release most of your hostages? I'll stay, of course, but my sister is just a teenager and the staff could leave while this is sorted out.'

Ghizlan tried and failed to repress the pounding thud of her heart at the thought of Mina at this man's mercy any longer. Mina was young and impulsive, and Huseyn al Rasheed didn't look like he had an understanding bone in his body.

'Sorted out? You speak as if I'm here temporarily. I assure you, *my lady*, that isn't the case. This is now my home.' His wide gesture encompassed not just the room, but the whole palace.

'Once the Council declares you Sheikh.'

'I expect that within a couple of days. I've already informed them of our impending marriage.'

Ghizlan's eyes popped. 'You had no right.'

'I had every right. I'm trying to save our country. Can't you see that?'

'What I see is a man so wrapped up in his bid for personal power he'll do anything to succeed.' It was a miracle she kept her voice even. Behind her back her knotted hands shook with the force of her outrage. 'I wouldn't be surprised to learn you had an army surrounding the city, ready to start a civil war.'

He stopped lounging against the desk. In the blink of

an eye he was standing tall, looming over her, his expression one of hauteur and repressed anger. 'I'll forgive that. *This time*. When you know me better you won't jump to such insulting assumptions.'

'I have no intention of knowing you better. You can't make me marry you.'

He didn't move, didn't lift a finger, but that smoky blue gaze grazed her face as surely as if he'd stroked rough fingers across her flesh. Beneath the whiskers his mouth curved in a slow smile that sent quivers of foreboding through her.

'If you're so set against it, *my lady*, so be it.' He paused. 'I'll simply marry your sister instead. Her royal blood is as good as yours. She's seventeen, is that right?' He paused, his smile widening. 'No doubt I'll find her much more *amenable* to my needs.'

For a second, then another and another, Ghizlan's heart stalled. Her stomach dropped sickeningly. She looked at the implacable man before her, read the determination in the set of his shoulders and the proud tilt of his head. The certainty in that complacent smile. And felt the world tremble on its foundations.

It was one thing for their father to try bartering Ghizlan into an arranged marriage to Sheikh Idris of Zahrat. At least Idris was a civilised, cultured, caring man. But to expect Mina, her innocent little sister, to marry this brute…

Ghizlan's arm swung up and she punched Huseyn al Rasheed full in the face.

CHAPTER FOUR

HUSEYN TURNED JUST in time. The blow glanced across his cheekbone an instant before his hand closed around hers, pulling it away from his face.

Just as well they didn't teach princesses boxing.

And that his reflexes were fast, honed by years of combat and training. She'd taken him by surprise and could have done some damage if she'd had a decent technique.

Huseyn stared into Ghizlan's flushed face. There was no mistaking the bloodlust in her burning eyes. If looks could kill he'd be six feet under.

Who'd have thought she had it in her to take him on?

His respect for her rose. Every minute in her presence she intrigued him more. The combination of ice and fire. The loyalty to and sense of responsibility for those who served her was unexpected too. His image of a self-absorbed socialite was fading fast.

But most of all, her courage amazed him. Huseyn knew grown men, trained soldiers, who'd retreat rather than fight him.

Heat scored his cheek where she'd made contact. Selim would laugh himself sick if he discovered an untrained woman had got past Huseyn's guard.

Serve you right for goading her. For expecting her to agree and make this easy. Since when has life been easy?

He'd had no compunction about threatening to marry Mina, in order to convince Ghizlan. This marriage was the key to success. He'd do whatever it took to keep his people safe.

But he'd been crass, acting like the sort of voluptuary he despised, as if he really wanted a teenager in his bed!

What was it about Ghizlan that made him sink so low? That made him taunt her again and again? He was no schoolboy, teasing a pretty girl to get her attention. This was about the fate of the nation, not some petty struggle for points.

Her eyes were over-bright—not with tears but fury. Her breasts thrust high with each panting breath and a shot of pure lust hit his belly, arrowing to his groin.

He wanted her. Like this. Full of fire and passion. Full of spark and spirit.

His fist closed more firmly around hers as he felt himself harden.

He wanted—

She winced, white teeth baring as she frowned. An instant later her face smoothed of expression.

That's when Huseyn realised how hard he gripped her hand. Instantly he released her, fingers spreading wide. 'My apologies. I didn't mean to hurt you.'

Perfect eyebrows arched on that fine forehead. 'You apologise for that but not for your threat to marry my little sister?'

Huseyn shrugged. Now he'd embarked on this course he had to follow through. 'Marriage to one of you will secure the throne quickly so I can protect Jeirut. It will ease tensions with other factions by providing a link to your father's rule. It's immaterial to me whether I marry you or your sister.'

Which was an outright lie.

Who'd bother with an adolescent when they could have Ghizlan?

She'd be trouble. She was too full of her own importance, too used to having her own way. But against that, she had pluck and more character than he'd expected. Plus a body made for pleasure. He wanted to haul her close and experience again the honey-cinnamon sweetness of her lips, and that unique dark, sultry flavour he'd found so addictive—the taste of her passion.

'Mina's a child!'

'She's seventeen. By law she's old enough to marry.'

'Only a brute would force someone so young into a marriage she doesn't want. Thanks to my father and grandfather we left those traditions behind long ago.'

Huseyn crossed his arms, noting the way her gaze skittered towards his chest. It was the sort of look women had been giving him ever since he'd grown out of puberty and it made him smile inside. She might pretend not to be attracted but the curiosity and the hunger were there, all right.

'Who says I'd be forcing her?'

Her lush lips tightened. 'You think you're irresistible?' She crossed her arms, mimicking his confrontational stance. But he'd bet she didn't realise it drew attention to the ripe curve of her breasts and the shadow of her cleavage. 'I've got news for you, Huseyn. Neither my sister nor I would be stupid enough to fall for a man like you.'

Her gazed raked him from head to toe, like a sergeant inspecting an unpromising recruit. He enjoyed her boldness. It was a new sensation. No woman had ever stood toe to toe against him. Instead they were only too eager to offer what he wanted.

'So you melting in my arms, kissing me as if you'd been starved for a man—that was you demonstrating how immune you are? Is that what you're saying?'

Her breath hissed and her eyes narrowed to slits of hatred that did nothing to diminish her attractiveness. Spitting fire or burning up in his embrace—both incarnations of Her Royal Bossiness were disturbingly enticing. And distracting. He needed to sort this wedding and move on.

'*Know your enemy* is a tried and true tactic.' Her chin shot up, drawing his eyes to the pale golden expanse of her throat. His pulse throbbed hard and low. He wanted to press his lips there again, taste the sweet spiciness of her flesh. And more.

Huseyn opened his arms wide, palms out, inviting her into his space. 'Feel free, *my lady*. I'm happy for you to *know* me in intimate detail if it will persuade you.'

She spluttered and he had to repress a grin. For all her hauteur she was amazingly easy to rile when the discussion turned to sex. Intriguing.

He beckoned her. 'Come. Don't be shy. It's a sacrifice I'm willing to make.'

'You're a cocky bastard, aren't you?'

He didn't hold back his grin then, surprised by her language. Who'd have thought to hear such words from the lips of such a fine lady?

'A bastard, yes, though my father took the trouble to legitimise me before he died.' His voice was bland, giving away none of his feelings on the fact that his father had waited over thirty years to do it. The old man had relied on him for years, had seen his promise early and cultivated it. Yet he'd never had any affection for the boy who'd come to him in rags and proven his loyalty again and again, usually by facing down dangers others baulked at. 'But cocky? No. I know my worth, probably more than the next man. I've spent my life proving it.'

Suddenly his good humour drained away. What did he think he was doing, playing word games with this woman? She had no notion how real people lived. People born in poverty. People living on a disputed border, where any night could bring marauders intent on pillage and death.

Huseyn let his arms drop to his sides.

'Know this, *my lady*. I intend to rule Jeirut and soon. That means marrying either you or your sister. No negotiation, no argument. I don't care if you believe I do it for my own prestige. I care even less if you think I'm a barbarian.'

He stepped forward, into her space, so her head jerked back. Though to her credit she stood her ground.

This time the tantalising honey scent of her skin only fired his impatience. He was more used to the scents of sweat and fear, of hard work and blood and dust. She was a distraction he didn't need.

'I'll give you till tomorrow morning to come to terms with that and agree to be my wife. If your answer is no, then I'll marry your sister instead.'

He paused, reading her fear, swiftly hidden. To his surprise he found himself lifting his hand, stroking a stray strand of hair back behind her ear, his hand big and rough against her silky perfection.

If he'd thought gentleness would win her over he was wrong. She shuddered beneath his touch, her body freezing in rejection. To her he was a savage. It was a timely reminder.

'I'll come for your answer at nine.'

Huseyn spun on his heel and left her.

'You're sure you know the way? We've been going for ages.' Mina's whisper came out of the cellar's darkness behind Ghizlan. Was that fear in her voice, or excitement?

Ghizlan hoped it was excitement. She was scared enough for the two of them after that climb across the sheer stone wall outside their windows. She hated heights. Even now she couldn't quell the sick terror in her belly after forcing herself out over her window ledge. Silently she cursed Huseyn al Rasheed and his thorough ways. The movement sensors on their doors meant the only escape had been out the windows and via the towering walls, which on their side of the palace dropped sheer to the valley below.

'I'm sure it's the way.' She forced the words through clenched teeth. 'It seems a long time because we're going slowly. But we need to save the light for later.' Without their phones they had no light source, save a single penlight torch Ghizlan had found in a drawer. But its light was dim and she didn't trust the battery to last. She'd save it for later.

'We're here.' Her hand, skimming the cold stone of the old cellar, found a corner, the wall turning at right angles. 'This is it!'

Relief coursed through her. After hours desperately considering and dismissing possible escape routes, the abandoned tunnel was their only hope. Cut through the living rock, the ancient passage into the city had been disused and forgotten for ages.

'Brilliant,' Mina whispered. 'This place gives me the creeps.' Light bloomed and Ghizlan blinked. Even the glow of the tiny torch was bright after the inky blackness. 'You need light to work the lock.'

If she could work it. As a child the ancient palace locks had fascinated her with their intricate, decorative metalwork. But it was a lifetime since Azim had shown her the secret to unlocking them. They'd been replaced by modern security devices. All, she hoped, except this one.

Her breath eased out as Mina played the torchlight further along the wall to a hefty door with massive hinges and a familiar, ancient lock.

Ghizlan's heart raced as she traced the metalwork, half-remembered instructions like whispers in her ears.

'Can you get it open?' Mina was at her shoulder.

'I can try.' Ghizlan sank to her knees, breathing deeply. She'd been only this height when Azim had shown her the trick—a lock that, despite the keyhole, didn't need a key if you were one of the very few who knew its secret.

Her fingers moved hesitantly, then with more confidence. There was a click as a hidden lever worked. A quiet curse and a frown as another refused to budge. Ghizlan gnawed at her lip, frowning as she tried and retried the various components. Had she got it wrong or had the lock seized from disuse? Cold sweat broke out between her shoulder blades at the idea they'd lost their one and only chance to escape. How could she protect Mina if—?

With a slow, grating groan, the pieces slid into place and the lock opened.

'You did it!' Mina's whisper was exultant.

Ghizlan stared, amazed she'd managed it. Amazed it had still been there. Luck was on their side. Until now she hadn't let herself actually believe.

'Come on. Let's get out of here.' Mina was already reaching for the huge twisted ring of metal on the door.

'No. Wait. Let me go first. We don't know for sure what's at the end of the tunnel and whether it's still open.' Mina started to protest but Ghizlan continued. 'I've been this way before. Let me test it first. One person will make less noise than two.'

Mina huffed. 'You think I'm still scared of spiders?'

It wasn't spiders Ghizlan had in mind. It was guards. She had no confidence the men Huseyn al Rasheed had brought would respect a pair of unprotected women if they came across them in the dark.

'If I'm not back in fifteen minutes, retrace your steps and go back to your room.'

'You're kidding, right?'

Ghizlan grabbed her sister's wrist, meeting her gaze. 'I'm serious. We don't know what we're walking into.' But she had to take this chance to spirit Mina away. 'Let me do this without arguing. Please?'

Finally Mina nodded, her defiance fading as she handed over the torch. 'Be careful.'

'You can count on it.' Then Ghizlan opened the door, wincing as the old hinges shrieked in the stillness. She switched off the light, her breath stopping as she slid through the door and pushed it almost shut behind her.

The air was different in the tunnel. Fresher? Hope rose but she made herself wait, listening. After a full minute she risked the torch, even then shielding it with her hand. What she saw made her heart leap. A bare tunnel fading into gloom. No blockages that she could see.

Switching off the light she moved to the side, fingertips touching the wall, and began to walk.

She counted three corners in the tunnel. Turning the last one she had to bite back a gasp of excitement. In the distance she saw a sprinkle of city lights, half hidden by what looked like undergrowth. She made herself wait, listening to her pulse pound erratically.

Finally, after waiting several minutes, Ghizlan sneaked to the end of the tunnel. Nothing. No sign of life except for the city's old quarter ahead. She'd go back and get Mina. But she had to be sure first.

Tucking the light into her pocket, she pushed aside a thorn bush, ignoring the darts of pain as it ripped at her hands and caught her clothes. Eyes closed to protect them, she groped her way, relief filling her as the last branches fell away and she stepped free.

Straight into something hard and warm and all too familiar.

Despair swamped her.

She should have known it couldn't be this easy.

Ghizlan's eyes snapped open as two large hands wrapped around her upper arms and tugged her off-balance. She had an impression of glinting eyes, then she landed against him, palms splayed on a muscled chest.

'Well, well, what have we here?' Huseyn al Rasheed's voice rumbled up beneath her hands, making her want to tug them free. *Feeling* that baritone as well as hearing it was far too intimate.

Frustrated tears prickled her eyes. They'd been so close to freedom.

'Stop squashing me!' Her breasts were pressed against him and she was surrounded by an earthy male scent. It was surprisingly appealing after the dank dustiness of the passage. No smell of horse this time, she noted. He must have had a shower.

She reared back. In the starlight she saw his smile. He

looked so complacent, so annoyingly unperturbed. It made her want to wipe that smile away.

'Is this how you get your jollies? Mauling women?'

The smile faded, replaced by a grim frown that made him look more formidable than ever. He thrust her back but still his huge hands shackled her shoulders.

Looming there in the dark he was big, hard and merciless. The hope she'd held like a flame inside flickered and died and Ghizlan tasted ashes on her tongue. Had she really believed she could spirit herself and Mina away from this man? He was like a genie in those old stories, the sort whose powers were unassailable. The sort who mocked the efforts of puny mortals to avoid their fate.

A shudder passed through her. Despite the lump of despair in her throat, Ghizlan met his stare head on. She might be defeated but she would go down fighting.

'You don't give up, do you?' He stared down into her tense face, wearily acknowledging the inevitability of tonight's little scene. He'd known from the first she was trouble with her defiance and that sinfully distracting body.

Of course it was too much to expect hoity-toity Princess Ghizlan to accept the inevitable gracefully. Especially when the inevitable included him, a low-born soldier, in her pristine bed. No doubt she saved that privilege for lovers as blue-blooded as she.

'Would you give up, in my position?' Her voice was low.

Damn her for stirring even a tickle of sympathy. This wasn't about her, or about him for that matter. It was about saving Jeirut from the bloodshed of war.

'I have better things to do with my night than bandy words with you, *my lady*. I don't appreciate being interrupted when I'm busy.' He'd been in the middle of crisis talks with some of the leaders eager to have him claim the throne. With luck they could bring this off quickly and—

'At two in the morning?' she sneered, her chin lifting

regally. 'Don't let me keep you. I hope she's a camp fol-
lower you brought from home and not someone from the
palace you forced into your bed.'

Huseyn's teeth ground together. She had a knack for
riling him—a man renowned for his patience.

'Careful, *my lady*. Even a despicable barbarian has his
pride. I'm tired of the implication the only way I can get
a woman into my bed is to force her.' He paused, letting
her see his displeasure. 'One more crack like that and I'll
begin to wonder at your interest in my sexual activities.'
Another pause, longer this time. 'I'd also be tempted to
demonstrate that no force is needed.'

Despite his anger, he felt the sizzle of erotic heat at the
thought of seducing Ghizlan. Though given the shimmering attraction he experienced whenever they got close he
wouldn't be surprised if they didn't make it to a bed.

For the first time since they'd met he'd reduced her to
speechlessness. He liked it.

'If you'll let me go—'

'What? You'll toddle off about your business?' He bent
forward, thrusting his face into her space. 'I think not.' He
sucked in the sweet honey scent he remembered from earlier and suddenly anger turned to burning fury.

'What the hell did you think you were doing, climbing
the outside wall of the palace? You could have fallen to
your death!' He hadn't wanted to believe the report when
it came through, except the guard in the corner tower was
one of Selim's best and he'd seen the two women with his
own eyes.

That had stopped Huseyn in his tracks—the idea the
women were so scared of him they'd risk their lives.

No, not scared of him. Scared of being forced to make a
sacrifice for their people instead of living in luxurious ease.

'Worried that you would be blamed?' Her eyebrows
rose scornfully.

'Worried you might have broken that pretty neck of

yours.' He dragged in another breath, trying to ignore the perfume of enticing female flesh beneath the scents of dust and clean sweat. Inevitably it made him wonder how she'd smell, and taste, burning up in ecstasy. 'You could have killed your sister too, or didn't that occur to you because you were too busy making your point?'

'Don't pretend you give a damn for Mina, or me.' He felt a shudder rack her body but she stood tall, her eyes glittering. 'All you care about is that it would be inconvenient if you had to scrape us up off the cliffs then explain why we'd fled for our lives.'

Huseyn drew in a calming breath. Then a second and a third. He'd grown used to people either obeying him or expressing gratitude for what he'd done for them.

It had been a long time since he'd faced vitriol. Not since he'd been a skinny, bastard kid, dependent on the unstable charity of his father for a roof over his head and food in his belly.

Deliberately he forced down the urge to do something reprehensible like turn her over his knee and spank her. It would relieve his tension but it would incite her to further recklessness. She had no concept how lucky she was to have lived in such privilege and safety, cosseted and protected.

'If you want to know what it's really like to fear for your life, go to my province of Jumeah and stay in one of the border villages. The Emir's men will strike there first when they attack Jeirut. Then you'll know real terror.' His voice was harsh with memories. Memories of arriving too late to prevent a fatal attack. And even older memories from early childhood, ones branded into his psyche. Of escaping such a raid by the skin of his teeth, only to discover his mother hadn't. 'Survive that, then talk to me about fear.'

That shut Ghizlan up. For once her scrutiny was all piercing curiosity with none of the dismissiveness that riled him.

'I'd like you to let me go now. Please.' It was said quietly, as if finally she acknowledged the urgency that drove him. 'I need to go back to my sister. She'll be worried.'

Huseyn forced breath from his lungs, dispelling the scent of blood and despair, as real as if the slaughter had just happened instead of decades ago.

Carefully he pulled his hands from Ghizlan's shoulders, surprised at his reluctance to release her. She was nothing but trouble. And yet...

'Your sister is being escorted to her room as we speak. Politely and with the utmost courtesy, of course.'

Ghizlan nodded curtly. 'Of course. I'd better go and see her.' Her voice was devoid of emotion but even in the starlight Huseyn read the slump of her shoulders.

He wanted to let her go, but he had to be sure there'd be no more lunatic escape attempts. Even now he couldn't quite believe the pair of them had found hand-and-footholds on the most forbidding face of a palace designed to withstand both bombardment and sneak assaults.

'I need your word you won't try to escape.'

Her laugh was brittle, like the scrape of icy fingers across his nape. 'I see no reason why I should give it.'

'It's either that, or I station a guard in each of your bedrooms.'

Her breath hissed in and her eyes bulged before narrowing to assessing slits. 'You really play dirty, don't you?' Disdain dripped from each syllable. At least she didn't waste her breath with protests that he wouldn't dare. He'd dare whatever it took.

'I don't *play, my lady*. I'm deadly serious. The sooner you learn life isn't a game the easier it will go for you.'

Surprisingly she didn't flinch away. She looked back steadily, her voice cool and crisp. 'I never had the luxury of believing it was. And the sooner *you* understand I'm not some brainless pawn you can use for your own ends, the better it will go with you. Interfering in people's lives has consequences. You may not like them.'

There was no bravado in her tone yet he heard the threat. Did she think he'd be scared to take her on because she was blue-blooded and born to privilege while he was a plain, honest soldier with only his honour and accomplishments to recommend him?

'That's a chance I'm willing to take.'

'And you'd take my word that we won't try to escape?' Disbelief tinged her tone.

'In the circumstances, yes.' He didn't try to explain his belief that however spoiled and wilful she might be, Princess Ghizlan had enough honour to abide by a promise. Her care for her people was proof of that.

'In that case you have my promise. Until tomorrow morning.' Her eyes never left his. She wasn't giving up.

She was destined to defeat, of course. But he'd be careful not to crush her spirit in the process. Despite her ability to infuriate him, he respected that in her.

With a flourish he gestured for her to proceed him on the path that led round the ramparts to the Palace's main entry. She pivoted on her heel and marched ahead, spine straight and head up, her slim figure intriguingly supple.

Huseyn swiped a hand over the back of his neck, rubbing at the muscles knotted there. He forced his gaze away from the fascinating, frustrating woman with her long-legged, hip-rolling stride and back to tonight's interrupted negotiations.

But it was difficult, more difficult than it should have been.

CHAPTER FIVE

GHIZLAN STRODE THROUGH the passage that led to the stables, her footsteps echoing on the old stones. She'd worn high heels, shiny black patent leather ones that screamed elegance and gave her a few precious inches of extra height. After a sleepless night she'd use whatever advantage she could get when facing Huseyn al Rasheed.

She still hated him. His behaviour appalled and his plans were unconscionable. But last night in the darkness when he'd spoken of fear, the bone-deep certainty in his voice, the realisation he wasn't posturing, had stopped her in her tracks.

He was power-hungry, selfish and brutal, yet she'd responded to the honesty he'd laid bare in the darkness last night. And to the surprising gift of his trust. There'd been no guard within or outside her room or Mina's last night and Mina was still sleeping, as cosy and safe as if there were no strangers patrolling the royal compound. For that at least, Ghizlan was grateful.

Huseyn al Rasheed was an annoying conundrum. A man she shouldn't take at face value. Yet part of her was tempted to think he actually believed what he said, outrageous and appalling as it was.

She twitched the jacket of her suit into place, scarlet this time, for courage. Another prop to help her with what promised to be the most difficult interview of her life.

Unless he'd changed his mind. She couldn't prevent the stray hope. It was past nine and he hadn't appeared in her father's study, apparently too busy in the stables to meet her to demand her answer. Maybe he didn't need a royal marriage after all.

Ghizlan pressed a palm to her sternum, trying to ease the pounding of her heart. She might be an optimist but she wasn't delusional. The chances of him changing his mind were microscopic. More likely he dallied in the stables as a way of putting her in her place, reinforcing how little he thought of her.

A loud whinny caught her ears, a crash and the quick thud of hooves. It was only then that she tuned in to the sound of male voices, sharp with warning and dismay.

She quickened her step, curious. Silence descended, broken only by the jingle of a harness and the percussion of hooves, staccato on the cobbles.

Turning a corner, Ghizlan reached one of the stable courtyards, surrounded by colonnades. Sunlight flooded down and she stood under one of the arches, blinking into the brightness.

Around the perimeter men loitered, intent on the courtyard. Hooves clattered and from one corner a giant horse pranced, chestnut coat gleaming in the sunlight, its muscles shifting with each deliberate, dance-like step. It tossed its head and a mane the colour of raw silk flared. On its back sat a horseman, broad-shouldered and straight-backed. He moved as if he were part of the magnificent beast—hands apparently relaxed, yet his hard thighs bunched beneath pale, dusty trousers and his white shirt was ripped half open across his chest as if he'd been in a brawl.

Without warning, the stallion's hindquarters bunched and it reared high, its eye rolling back towards its rider. There was a gasp from the crowd but the rider clung on, leaning forward as if whispering to it. Mighty hooves thudded down with a clang that struck sparks, then the horse was flying, bucking and wheeling in a desperate attempt to dislodge his rider.

Reflexively Ghizlan stepped back as the pair thundered past. In the flurry of movement one impression lingered— the smile on the rider's face. On Huseyn al Rasheed's face.

A smile of absolute delight, as if battling a horse who wanted to trample him underfoot was the most marvellous treat.

Her breath caught. That smile, the sight of such unadulterated joy, sent unexpected sensations hurtling through her. Energy zapped and adrenalin pulsed. Not just from the danger of what she witnessed, but because of the blinding white grin on the face of the man she abhorred.

Another step took her back till she leant against a pillar, heart pounding. She was still reeling when, with a whinny that might have been defiance or perhaps defeat, the stallion finally dropped to stand docile, its ears flicking, its heavy breaths and twitching muscles the only reminders of its earlier battle.

Huseyn al Rasheed leaned forward, his square hand caressing the animal's neck, and Ghizlan could swear it listened to every word. Finally, with no apparent order from its rider, the stallion stepped neatly and quietly towards a groom waiting in the shadows. With one final pat, Huseyn dismounted and the horse was led away, docile as if there'd been no bloodlust in its eyes as it had tried to unseat its rider.

Ghizlan had never seen anything like it. Whatever else he might be, her tormentor was a horseman of immense skill.

Better to focus on that than Huseyn's smile. Its impact had seared her—a tangible assault.

The groom said something and Huseyn spun round, his smile dying.

She told herself she was glad. She didn't want to like anything about him. Not his infectious smile. Not his sheer, stupid joy at risking his neck on that brute of a horse. Not even his incredible horsemanship.

The onlookers faded back into the stables and he crossed the dusty courtyard with a loose-limbed stride that reminded her not of a soldier this time but an athlete. Maybe that was because his torn shirt revealed part of a powerful, hair-smattered chest that would have done a weightlifter proud. Ghizlan's pulse gave a little dance of feminine appreciation. Her eyes bulged before she forced them up to meet his misty blue gaze. It was like the sky over the mountains after dawn, clear and cool and totally impersonal. As if nothing untoward had happened. As if there'd been no danger.

'You could have killed yourself! Have you no sense at all?' Ghizlan wasn't aware of forming the words until they rang out. She blinked and bit back whatever else was on her tongue.

He halted, frowning. The sunshine turned his tousled hair blue-black, a glossy invitation. To her horror Ghizlan felt a corresponding tingle in her fingers and bunched them tight.

'You were concerned about me?' He looked as stunned as she.

He stood before her, huge, dusty and dishevelled, a smear of blood along the tear on his shirt and a look of disbelief on his face. And all she could think about was the raw, gut deep horror tightening her insides at the idea of him lying lifeless on the cobblestones. It was absurd. Appalling.

'Of course not! What do I care if you break that thick skull of yours? It would solve a lot of problems. I just…' She paused, her words petering out. She breathed deeply, ignoring the scent of horse and clean male sweat that she'd already told herself she couldn't possibly like, and lifted her chin. 'It would leave me to deal with your rabble of followers.'

'Ah. My followers.' He nodded, black curls slipping against his collar. 'You mean the highly trained, completely disciplined soldiers who managed to outmanoeuvre your so-called security staff without a single blow? You were

worried they'd panic and run amok if they saw my dead
body?'

Then he smiled, damn him. A slow, drawn-out smile
that stretched his mouth wide and spoke of pure amusement. Amusement at *her*. He was laughing at her because
she'd been stupid enough to express concern for him, her
enemy.

Or was he laughing because he'd somehow sensed her
response to his powerful, masculine body?

Anger flooded her. It was bad enough he'd captured the
palace with such ease and that he held everyone here at
his mercy. The humiliation of his laughter was too much.

'You think it funny?' She stepped forward, into his
space, pleased when his smile slid away and surprise tightened those bold features. 'To be at the mercy of a bunch of
armed men isn't my idea of fun, nor my sister's. You might
think them wonderful but I see a bunch of cowards who
overcame men far better than themselves by threatening to
harm my sister.' She folded her arms over her chest. 'The
sort of men who would hold an innocent girl to ransom
aren't ones I could trust.'

His amusement was gone now. His face was like flint,
those cheekbones craggy beneath lowering brows.

'Come.' His hand closed round her upper arm. 'This
isn't the place for this conversation.'

To Ghizlan's annoyance, even in heels she didn't reach
his eye level. When he spun her back towards the corridor
she was surrounded by his hot, strong body and spicy scent.
She dug her heels in until he stopped, scowling down at her.

'I'm not a sack of potatoes to be dragged from place
to place. You only have to ask me to move, not grab me.'
She paused, catching her breath. 'Besides, you're the one
who didn't have the courtesy to meet me at nine. I had to
come looking for you.'

'And in the stables of all places. How that must have

irked your fastidious soul.' His gaze was provocative. 'How far beneath your royal person.'

It was on the tip of her tongue to burst out that she'd once spent hours in the stables. That in her teens riding had been her passion. Until her father had decreed she needed to focus on other, more useful activities, like acting as his hostess, studying and learning to serve their people.

'Does this mean you're ready to talk now? Or does your leisure time take precedence?' She let her gaze sweep him as coolly as if her pulse wasn't doing a crazy double-quick beat. She was determined to conquer this awareness of him as a man. It was simply that, despite meeting men all the time, she'd never met one so unabashedly, so in-your-face *male*. Or one whose lingering stare wasn't at all respectful but held a heat she distrusted.

'If you're ready, *my lady*.' He didn't acknowledge her jibe. With an ostentatious deliberation that mocked her title, he lifted his hand from her arm and put space between them. Pity he couldn't also erase the burning awareness where his hand had clamped her upper arm.

'I'm ready.'

She turned and led the way, conscious of the click of her heels on the stone floor and the curious sensation that skated from her upswept hair, down her spine to her legs then back up again. His stare did that. She didn't know how. She didn't want to know. But she was conscious of it with every step.

It was that awareness, that claustrophobic sense of being tethered to the man behind her, unable to escape, that led her not to her father's study but to a balcony that hung out over the valley below. On this side, away from the city, the wall dropped to the escarpment's sheer cliffs and, if she wanted to make herself sick, she only had to lean forward to see the hazardous route she and Mina had taken last night. She'd never have dared it in daytime. Thinking about it made her feel queasy.

Instead she planted her hands on the balustrade, sucking fresh mountain air into tight lungs. She kept her eyes fixed on the vast desert sprawling from the foothills as far as the eye could see.

'You have an answer for me?' That deep baritone rolled along her bones, shivering into recesses she tried to hide.

'About marrying you?'

'What else?'

Another slow, fortifying breath. She didn't turn to him. This would be easier if she didn't look at him.

If only she could avoid him totally.

Desperate humour stirred at the thought of a bride wanting never to lay eyes on her groom. That would suit her perfectly.

'My lady?' For once she heard no sarcasm when he used her title. Somehow that made this moment even more horribly real.

'*If* I were to agree to marry you I'd have conditions.'

'Go on.'

'First, my sister leaves the country before the wedding.'

'Immediately after.'

'Not good enough.'

'You don't trust me to make good on my promise?' He sounded like a grumbly bear.

'You've done nothing to earn my trust.' Ghizlan focused on a distant blue, razorback ridge rising from the desert. As a child she'd imagined it was the spine of a sleeping dragon. She could do with a dragon right now—some powerful creature to save her and Mina.

But there was no one who could save Mina. Only her.

'I kept my word last night. There were no guards posted at your rooms.'

'True. But even you must see this isn't in the same league. The only way I'd consider this…arrangement is if I know Mina will be free.' Her hands clenched on the balustrade so hard the grit from the ancient stone bit into her palms.

'You have my word as Sheikh of Jumeah.' He paused as if waiting. When she didn't respond he continued. 'On my honour. And my mother's memory.'

Doubt tickled Ghizlan. She knew he was a warrior who took claims to honour seriously. But to promise on his mother's memory, rather than his father's? What did that say about his relationship with the old Sheikh?

'I'll have a plane standing by to take her wherever she wants to go.'

'France. She wants to go to France.' Suddenly it hit Ghizlan that, if she did give in to this man, it might be years before she saw Mina again. She blinked and focused on maintaining a mask of calm while inside she crumbled.

'France then.'

'As soon as the ceremony is over.' She swung around and met that silvery blue stare. She told herself it was as cold and unemotional as ice, yet the shiver racing through her was hot, not icy.

'Agreed.'

'And there'll be no attempt to freeze our bank accounts.'

A frown pleated that wide brow. She could see him wondering how vast a fortune they had salted away. Maybe it would be simpler to explain that was far from the truth, that since the age of sixteen they'd both lived off modest inheritances left by their respective mothers. The royal treasury paid only for official travel and the lavish gowns required for formal court occasions.

'Agreed.'

'And—'

'You've already negotiated enough concessions.'

Ghizlan let her eyebrows arch in a show of astonishment. 'I hardly see the right to travel and to keep our own possessions as any sort of concession. In a civilised environment they would go without saying.'

His eyes narrowed to glacial slivers. She couldn't be sure because of the whiskers, but she suspected he was grinding his teeth. The notion gave her confidence.

'Four more points only.'

'Four?' He scowled down at her. 'Well, spit them out.'

'You release every prisoner you've taken. Unharmed.'

He nodded. 'I'd planned to. *After* the wedding.'

Ghizlan opened her mouth to argue for their immediate release then decided it was better to accept the compromise and continue.

'Mina and I have access to our email accounts from this moment.'

'That I can't allow.'

'Because we'll foment trouble?' She shook her head. 'I have no interest in bloodshed. But I have several commercial matters that need attention. And Mina is expecting news that will determine her future.' Ghizlan knew her sister's talent. Surely it was enough to secure a place at the art school she'd set her heart on. If not, Ghizlan would investigate sponsoring her somewhere else.

His gaze grew assessing and Ghizlan found herself holding her breath. She hated that she had to go cap in hand to this man for the favour of continuing her work.

'Very well,' he said at last. 'But under supervision.'

'Impossible. We need our privacy.'

'I thought you said it was about commercial matters.' His tone dripped disbelief and it hit Ghizlan he had no idea of her work. What had he called her? A pampered waste of space? He probably thought she used the net to gossip with girlfriends instead of initiating projects to improve the lives of her people and open up new opportunities.

She could try explaining about the state-of-the-art waste water systems in provincial towns, the nation's first pharmaceutical factory being built on the far side of the capital and her other pet project, still in the design phase. But a glance at his expression told her he wouldn't believe her.

'How about a compromise? We read our messages privately, but any responses are vetted before sending?'

'Done. That's two points. What are the other two?'

'That I'll be free to go about my business unhindered.' Ghizlan refused to live under perpetual house arrest.

His gaze scrutinised her so sharply she'd swear she felt it scrape her cheeks. 'On condition that your behaviour befits the wife of the royal Sheikh.'

Did he imagine her living a life of debauchery? Ghizlan was torn between the desire to laugh and the desire to smack his face. She'd never in her life been violent before meeting Huseyn al Rasheed. He evoked frighteningly primitive responses, even in a woman who'd spent her life learning to be proper at all times.

'You think I'd drag your name through the gutter?' For a moment the idea tempted.

He shook his head. 'I wouldn't allow it.' There was no doubt in that deep, decisive tone. He believed himself her master. The idea irked more than anything else.

Ghizlan sucked in a deep breath, willing herself not to snap out a response she'd regret. She needed his agreement. She couldn't lose her temper now.

Yet her voice, when she found it, was brittle. 'I have a far better idea than you of what's appropriate behaviour for the royal Sheikh's consort. Believe me, I have no intention of sullying my father's memory or my own good name just to make life difficult for you.'

She'd spent her entire life hemmed in by duty, behaving as a proper princess should, responsibly, courteously, always gracious and calm. If anyone was taking a wrecking ball to the royal reputation it was this arrogant lout.

He had no idea how important her work was, and how much went on behind the scenes to ensure the royal court and the administration ran like clockwork. Huseyn al Rasheed thought leading was about macho posturing and armies and telling people what to do.

He'd learn.

'What are you smiling about?' His eyes narrowed to slits of suspicion.

Her own eyes widened innocently. 'I'm just waiting for your agreement.' When he said nothing she hurried on. 'The people will expect to see me about as usual. It will be a sign that everything's okay and there's been a peaceful handover of power.' The idea choked her and she had to pause and swallow.

'Very well. You'll be free, within the borders of Jeirut. But your security detail will report your movements to me and if I discover anything inappropriate...' His expression was grim and Ghizlan knew a moment of fear, wondering what he'd do if roused to fury. Lock her in a dungeon and throw away the key? 'And your last item, my lady? What is it?'

Ghizlan forced down a sudden thickness in her throat. She'd come this far. She would succeed with this too. She had to. Ruthlessly she squashed those betraying nerves. She let go her hold on the balustrade and tilted her chin to meet his stare head on.

'When the time comes you won't stand in the way of our divorce.'

His dark brows scrunched together. 'When the time comes?'

She huffed out an impatient breath. Surely it was simple enough. 'Once the people have time to accept you and you're established as Sheikh you won't need me any more. You only need me for the transition from my father's reign.' Ghizlan paused, swallowing yet again. She hoped he didn't notice. 'Once that happens you won't want me cluttering up your life. I'll leave and you can choose a wife who suits you better.' Someone biddable and obedient. Beautiful, no doubt, petite and delicate. Someone impressed by his muscles and his masterful air. Someone who wanted nothing more than a man to tell her how to live her life.

Someone not at all like her.

Why the thought disturbed, she didn't know.

Still he didn't respond. That hint of a frown lingered and his nostrils looked pinched. In anger or contemplation? Surely he saw the sense in a clean break?

Finally he nodded and relief was a warm rush, weakening her knees so she put out a hand onto the warm stonework beside her. She'd been strung tight as an archer's bow.

'When I don't need you any more we'll divorce. Is that all?'

Ghizlan nodded. For the life of her she couldn't form the words.

'Good. We'll be married by the end of the week.'

She opened her mouth to protest, saw his expectant look, then shut it again. The end of the week was two days away. She needed more time—to get used to the idea of this objectionable marriage, or to plan a better escape.

A large hand grabbed hers, engulfing then shaking it. Huseyn's gesture was disconcerting. She felt the heat of his flesh, the ridge of calluses across his palm, the surprisingly neat fit of her hand in his big paw. It should have been businesslike, a mere confirmation of their verbal agreement.

Except for the rippling arc of power traversing her body, like circles of waves around a stone dropped in a still pool. Tiny sparks flared under her skin and warmth flushed her throat and face. She hated the insidious awareness he created in her.

She'd hoped to avoid touching him again. The press of his flesh against hers evoked haunting, devastating memories of that kiss. Of how she'd given up fighting and instead capitulated in humiliating eagerness. As if she wanted this man's attention. His touch. His passion.

She backed up a step, tugging her hand free, uncaring whether he read her discomfort.

'Until the wedding.' He nodded once then spun on his heel and strode into the building.

Ghizlan fell back against the sun-warmed stone. What had she expected? To see delight on those sombre features? To hear his thanks for the sacrifice she made?

He'd got what he wanted and that was all he cared about.

The sooner she learned to expect absolutely nothing from her husband-to-be, the better. He didn't like her and she detested him. She intended to see as little of him as possible until the day came for their divorce.

CHAPTER SIX

HUSEYN'S GAZE SWEPT the royal audience chamber. They were all here. Every member of the Royal Council, each provincial sheikh, government minister and senior office holder. Every leader whose opinion counted when it was time to proclaim the new Sheikh.

Some were exuberant, some grim, but all, it seemed, content to wait and see if it was true that Princess Ghizlan had promised to wed him and therefore support him as Royal Sheikh.

Anger stirred his belly. Already there'd been skirmishes on the border. Already men risked their lives, fending off the Emir of Halarq's raiding parties. Huseyn knew how he worked. He was testing Jeirut's defences. But any day now he'd make his move, pushing hard and fast over territory where for generations Huseyn's people had lived.

He was tired of the interminable waiting. Of negotiating and hand-holding nervous old men who should have been pensioned off years ago, and young ones who had no concept of real danger. He wanted to—

A ripple passed through the crowd. About time. He'd been about to send someone to fetch her. Ghizlan had left it until the last possible moment to make her appearance. The guards at the door stepped neatly aside and two women entered. The first was slim and coltish, dressed in muted tones. The second—

Huseyn's breath stalled as Ghizlan strode into the room. She didn't look like any bride he'd ever seen. She looked confident, statuesque as a proud goddess, full of a blazing energy he felt even from across the room.

Head up and stiletto heels clicking an assured rhythm

in the pin-drop silence, she looked regal and powerful and beautiful enough to stop a man's pulse.

She was magnificent. Superb.

Her hair was piled high in some elaborate, elegant arrangement that complemented her tiara of flashing silver-blue fire. Diamonds and sapphires, he guessed. But they were nothing to the bright glint in her eyes as she surveyed the throng grouped in clusters around the room.

Her chin lifted higher as she crossed the marble floor, her sister in tow now, heading directly for him.

Huseyn had never appreciated the sight of a woman as much as he did now.

And soon she'd be his.

No traditional wedding veils for his bride. No long skirts sweeping the floor. No fluttering hennaed hands. Neither did she wear a Western-style wedding dress of white. He hadn't really expected that, but neither had he expected *this*.

His belly clenched hard on itself as she marched across the vast space and he reacted with pure male appreciation.

Flouting tradition, as he'd guessed she would, Ghizlan wore Western dress. A dress that clung to her ripe, perfect body, making her stride a symphony of lush breasts and rounded hips and a waist narrow enough to dry his throat. His palms tingled with the desire to touch and fire wound its way through his bloodstream, tangling with adrenalin in a combustible mix.

The dress ended at her knees, but the subtle sheen of the fabric highlighted long, slender thighs with each step she took. Then there were those calves, shapely in break-neck heels.

Sex on legs. But she was more. Far more.

Power and disdain and absolute challenge.

For his bride hadn't chosen to wear gold or red, the traditional colours for rejoicing. She'd avoided colour completely on this auspicious day. Instead her wedding dress was of rich, velvety black. The colour of mourning.

And she wore what he guessed were royal heirloom jewels at her wrists, throat, ears and hair with a nonchalance that reminded everyone present of her impeccable aristocratic lineage.

Huseyn's lips twitched as she stopped before him. He wanted to applaud her defiance and her courage. Her disdain for him. Her disdain for the crowd of men filling the room who must guess, if they didn't know for sure, that she was here under coercion, yet who did nothing to assist her.

He looked into eyes glittering with pride and defiance and felt something rise inside. Something more than mere lust.

Appreciation. Respect.

Huseyn stepped back on one foot, bowing deeply in a gesture not just of courtesy but of deference.

'My lady. You do me great honour.' He lifted his head and caught a flash of surprise before her face smoothed into an imperturbable, regal mask. 'I've never had the pleasure of seeing such a striking, truly beautiful woman.' For in this moment Ghizlan outclassed every woman he'd ever known. And he'd known a few.

He reached out and took her unresisting hand. Closing his fingers around hers. Her pulse hammered beneath the soft skin at her wrist and his admiration notched higher. Not even by a flicker of expression did she betray her nerves.

If he had to have a wife he'd far rather one like this—one with fire—than all the submissive, eager women he'd known.

He lifted her hand and pressed his lips to her flesh, inhaling the cinnamon-honey scent of her skin, lingering to enjoy the taste of her.

* * *

Ghizlan stared at the man bending over her hand with such courtly gallantry. She had to fight not to goggle.

This couldn't be Huseyn al Rasheed, the arrogant Iron Hand of Jumeah. The man who revelled in boorish aggression and macho posturing.

He exuded suave sophistication in a formal suit that fitted so perfectly it could only have been tailored by a master. Fine fabric clung to broad shoulders and long legs, creating a mouthwatering display of male confidence.

Yet the Western clothes, so surprising in a man of such deliberate barbarism, couldn't hide his essential power.

Ghizlan felt it in the light clasp of his big hand. More, in the spark of response shivering through her from the touch of those warm lips on her skin. She hauled in a breath redolent of shock and testosterone and fought down panic.

He was daunting enough with his beard and traditional horseman's garb. Shaved and dressed like this...

'There's no need to make a spectacle of us both.' She jerked her hand from his grip, rubbing her other palm over the spot where his mouth had pressed her flesh, as if to erase the imprint of his touch.

Slowly he straightened, standing close enough that she had to crane her neck to meet his eyes. More blue than grey today, if she didn't know better she'd say they looked almost approving. The idea made her pulse jerk waywardly.

One jet eyebrow flicked high. 'I was merely according you the formal courtesy you deserve, my lady.' His gaze dipped to the weight of diamonds draping her neck, then lower, to the black velvet that now seemed unaccountably stifling despite the chill of the vast, high-ceilinged space. 'As for a spectacle...' His lips, long and well shaped, curled in a smile she *felt* in her belly, 'I leave that to you.' He lifted his eyes. 'You're magnificent.'

It sounded like a compliment. Except she knew better than to believe it.

Ghizlan had entered the hall full of bravado yet he'd pulled the rug out from beneath her feet.

She swallowed. Hard. No man's smile did that to her. Ever.

Yet, bereft of his beard, he looked less like a merciless marauder and more like a movie star. Not the cute boy-next-door types who'd done so well in recent years, but the red-blooded, swoonworthy ones who could seduce a woman with a smile while fighting off a villain and single-handedly foiling a plot to destroy the planet. Even that broken nose added to his charisma, to the aura of strength and masculinity he exuded.

An aura that turned her poised defiance into a jumble of warring emotions and made her wonder if she'd bitten off more than she could chew, conceding to this wedding. Fear gnawed at her.

In a flash her flesh was prickling at the memory of his mouth on hers, his arms locked around her, body pressed close. Heat licked her insides, sending shivery hot chills through her taut body.

His jaw was as strong as she'd guessed, square and dependable-looking. What she hadn't guessed was the intriguing hint of a cleft in his chin, and the long dimples that creased his cheeks when he smiled.

She blinked. Dimples? Impossible. But still they showed, grooves of pleasure as he smiled down at her, eyes dancing. Frantically she scanned his face. It was still hard, still honed and strong, but that glow of amusement transformed him from beast to human, from bogeyman to hunk.

Ghizlan cleared her throat. It didn't matter how he looked or how elegant his bow. He was a thug. 'I didn't expect to see you in a suit.' Her voice grated. 'Surely you're all about old-fashioned values and traditions.' She paused, tugging in a sustaining breath. 'Like treating women as chattels.'

His smile shut off instantly. Yet for once she was spared his forbidding scowl. Instead he looked merely sombre.

'Perhaps I wanted to match you.'

Ghizlan said nothing, reminding herself he'd had no way of knowing for sure what she'd wear. He'd at least kept his promise and left her and Mina alone to prepare for today. There'd been no guards, no spies in their apartments.

'Or maybe you wanted to make a point of appearing as something more than a leader from a rustic province.' His expression didn't change but something in his eyes told her she was on the right track. 'That's it. You're trying to look the part of a national leader! Someone who can work in an international setting.'

Of course he was. Despite the fact not one of the throng of onlookers made any attempt to stop this farce of a wedding, she knew some among them doubted Huseyn's ability to rule the nation and deal in international relations.

She kept her voice low as she let her lips curve into a cold smile. 'It will take more than a well-tailored suit to turn *you* into a diplomat.'

Annoyingly he didn't seem to register her jibe. Instead he smoothed one large hand down the lapel of his jacket. 'You approve? I'll be sure to inform my tailor. Since he's from a *rustic* province, he'll be delighted to have praise from someone with such expertise in fashion.'

Amusement still lurked in his eyes but there was no mistaking his implication—that her knowledge was shallow, all about fripperies, while his masculine understanding was practical and important.

Obviously he knew nothing about her. If she didn't already detest the man she'd be incensed he hadn't bothered to research her—just assumed her role was decorative and her interests lightweight.

That showed how little he understood the work behind

the scenes to bring about the progress for which her country was admired. But he'd learn. Ruling a nation was hard work and it needed more than a soldier's skills.

His narrowing eyes told her he'd read something in her expression and Ghizlan smoothed out her features. She glanced to one side where Mina stood a little apart, hands gripped tightly together, and instantly shoved aside thoughts of beating him in a verbal battle. What did that matter when her sister's future was on the line?

She took a half step closer, ignoring the tantalising scent of fresh male skin. 'You promise you'll let Mina leave?'

'I gave my word, didn't I?'

The trouble was Ghizlan didn't know if that was enough. This man was renowned for adhering to an old-fashioned warrior code, where personal honour ranked high. Yet in the circumstances, where he held every advantage... Was she mistaken to believe he'd release Mina when she was a hostage to Ghizlan's good behaviour? How ruthless was he? Ruthless enough to stage a coup rather than wait for due process to be named her father's heir. Ruthless enough to break his word to a woman he viewed as a waste of space?

Abruptly heat engulfed her as a callused hand wrapped around hers, completely enfolding it.

Startled, she looked up into eyes the colour of the desert sky after dawn, when the first sheen of pale blue washed it clear.

'Stop fretting.' His deep voice was soft. Oddly, Ghizlan found its timbre reassuring as it resonated through her. 'Your sister will be fine.'

She opened her mouth but before she could speak his grip tightened and he turned towards their audience. 'Come, it's time we got this wedding over.'

Firmly she repressed a shudder of apprehension. If this was what it took to free her sister, she'd do it and be damned if she'd let the cowards surrounding her guess at her anguish. She set her chin and stepped forward.

Ghizlan stood on the tarmac, feeling the cool evening breeze stream by, and worked to keep a smile on her stiff features. She didn't know which was worse, needing to keep up a show of calm encouragement for Mina, or having her new husband watch everything that passed between them.

Even now, as she kissed her little sister and forced herself to step back, she was acutely aware of him looming nearby. As if he didn't trust her not to make a dash for the plane that would fly Mina to France and safety.

Or more probably for the benefit of the onlookers on the edge of the tarmac. There were cameras trained on them and Ghizlan assumed he was making a point of looking like a supportive spouse.

'I'll be fine,' Mina whispered. 'You don't have to worry about me, really.' Her glance darted sideways. 'But will you, Ghizlan? I don't like leaving you.'

Ghizlan shook her head sharply. 'I'll be okay. I'm going to be the royal Sheikha, remember? Besides, there's no point both of us staying. You've got a chance to do what you love and—'

'And what about you? Don't you deserve—?'

Ghizlan raised her hand. 'It was my choice, Mina.' She hadn't told her sister of Huseyn's threat to marry her instead if Ghizlan refused. 'With me here there's a good chance this transition of authority will go smoothly. If I can help keep the peace…' She shrugged. 'It's my duty to do what I can.'

Mina frowned. 'You've done your duty all these years. You—'

Movement beside her made Ghizlan turn. It was Huseyn, his face inscrutable as he approached. 'It's time.'

Beyond him the cabin steward was waiting at the bottom of the steps to the plane.

Ghizlan swallowed a knot of emotion and wrapped her arms around her little sister as Mina leaned in for another hug. 'Don't forget—'

'I know, I know. I'll call you as soon as I'm settled. And I'll ring regularly. And I'll see Jean-Paul for you too and find out how he's going.'

Ghizlan smiled, ignoring the way her cheeks felt pulled too tight by stress. 'Perfect. Tell him I can't wait to hear from him.'

Then Mina was walking away, her baby sister suddenly almost grown up. Yet Ghizlan couldn't help worry about how she'd cope, living away from home for the first time.

'She'll be all right.' To her surprise, the deep burr of Huseyn's voice was surprisingly reassuring.

Ghizlan nodded, her throat tight. She lifted her hand as Mina reached the top of the stairs onto the plane and turned to wave. 'Of course she will.' Yet worry gnawed at her belly.

'I've asked the ambassador to check on her from time to time in Paris. And a friend of mine, a professor at the Sorbonne, is going to invite her to lunch to meet his family. He has teenagers so with luck they may strike up a friendship.'

Ghizlan spun round, her brow crinkling. *She'd* already asked the Jeiruti Ambassador to France to look out for Mina. And Huseyn had done it too? 'You did?' Wasn't all his effort focused on grabbing the sheikhdom?

This wasn't the action of a self-serving thug. It was thoughtful and reassuring. As if he genuinely cared about how her little sister fared.

'Don't look so surprised. She's my sister now.' One eyebrow rose interrogatively. 'Or is it the fact I know anyone as civilised as a professor of languages?'

Both, actually.

Did he really consider himself bound to look after Mina?

The idea of this man in the role of protector was so novel Ghizlan knew she was gawking but she couldn't help it. First his exquisitely tailored suit. Then an act of thoughtfulness.

Had some genie spirited Huseyn al Rasheed away and replaced him with a changeling?

'No, don't answer that. I can guess.' Despite the glimmer of amusement in his eyes, his mouth tightened.

For a single moment the ridiculous idea surfaced that he was disappointed in her reaction. Except that was too patently farcical.

'That's very kind of you,' she said through stiff lips as he took her arm and turned her towards their limousine. Instantly little darts of heat fizzed out from his touch, making her skin tingle and her breath seize.

In the distance there was a flurry of activity as the photographers jockeyed for the best shot of them.

That explained why he touched her, and why he'd made the gesture of concern for Mina—he had a vested interest in them looking like a real couple rather than a brute with his forced bride. The fiction of a solid marriage would help him get what he really wanted—the throne. Everything he did was calculated to achieve that goal.

The knowledge stiffened her backbone and chilled her blood as she marched towards the car. She'd married a man she abhorred and—

'Who's Jean-Paul?'

'Sorry?' She stumbled and he hauled her closer so his heat enveloped her as her hip brushed his thigh. A flutter of unfamiliar sensation turned her pulse to a staccato throb.

'Jean-Paul.' His voice was soft but taut. 'The man you're so desperate to hear from. Is he a lover?'

Ghizlan swung her head round to meet a piercing silvery stare. The trained scientist in her wondered how it could be that his eyes appeared to change colour with his temper. But mainly she was intrigued at his interest. Because he didn't want her doing anything that undermined the fiction of their marriage—like flaunt a lover?

Jean-Paul was old enough to be her grandfather and their relationship, though friendly, was based on business. He was the key to her new venture to revitalise the ancient perfume industry in Jeirut and give it a modern twist that would bring money and work to people eager to better themselves.

She let her lips curve in a slow smile. 'I have no intention of questioning you about your love life, neither do I intend to share any such personal information with you.'

Those long fingers tightened around her upper arm. No mistaking his annoyance.

Ghizlan experienced a flare of unholy delight to have scored even such a small point over the man who'd stormed into her life, taking it over as if she had no right to choose for herself. She might not be able to escape him but there was pleasure in reminding him she was no pushover.

'Afraid it would take you too long in the telling?' His lips widened in what might, at a distance, look like a smile, but which, up close, was no more than a baring of strong, white teeth. Like a mountain wolf eyeing off a juicy lamb.

Ghizlan swallowed hard but refused to look away. She refused to feel fear. No matter how…carnivorous the look he sent her. Besides, the alternative, telling him she didn't have a love life and never had, was unthinkable.

'Isn't it time we headed back?' She shot a glance at the limo waiting for them. 'You don't want to miss your wedding feast, not with all those important people you want to impress.'

Huseyn gritted his teeth as he handed his new bride into the car. He couldn't believe how easily she provoked him. As for the slivers of hot metal pricking at him when he thought of her with her French lover…

His jaw locked as he identified the unfamiliar sensation.

Jealousy.

Impossible, remarkable, unlooked for. He'd never been jealous of a woman in his life. Never cared about one enough to be bothered.

But it was true. The blurred image in his brain of Ghizlan writhing in the arms of some suave Frenchman churned his gut and made him want to lash out. If Jean-Paul were here Huseyn would take pleasure in thrashing him.

Stunned by the well of fury simmering so close to the surface, Huseyn took his time walking to the other side of the car. It was normal, he reassured himself, to feel possessive about his wife, even if they'd only been married an hour. Even if they didn't really want each other.

Ghizlan was his now and what was his he kept. He had no intention of sharing her.

Everything he had was hard won and he valued it. Even his unwilling spouse. *Especially* his unwilling, hauntingly provocative, endlessly fascinating wife.

He should be devising tactics to deal with the power-brokers attending the wedding feast yet instead he was fixated on the possibility his wife had planned a rendezvous with another man.

Huseyn shook his head. Feisty she might be, but she'd met her match. There'd be no other lovers. Not while she was his.

On that satisfying thought he took the seat beside her and reached to take her hand, knowing it unsettled her. It wasn't because he enjoyed the feel of her soft palm fitting snugly against his, or the quiver that passed through her—evidence of the searing attraction she tried so hard and yet failed every time to hide. He knew enough about women to recognise attraction when he met it. No, Huseyn was simply reminding her that she belonged to him now.

'I look forward to having you at my side as we celebrate with our guests, *my lady.*' As ever, she stiffened further, correctly reading the thread of amusement as he used her title.

'I'm glad one of us is looking forward to it,' she huffed, turning her head away to look out the window.

But her fighting spirit didn't annoy him. Not when he held her hand and felt the fast, trembling pulse beating at her wrist. Not when he knew, for all her blustering, it was excitement as much as nerves, winding her so tight.

He'd enjoy helping her unwind.

CHAPTER SEVEN

HER MAID HAD laid out a nightgown for her. It lay demurely stretched across the counterpane—ruby silk with panels of delicate lace. Ghizlan stared at it for a full thirty seconds before swiping it off the bed and stuffing it in a drawer.

First, her maid had never before chosen her nightwear and she wasn't about to start now.

Second, the gesture was clearly designed to help her seduce her new husband. Which she wasn't going to do under any circumstances. He'd be sleeping wherever it was he'd slept since he'd arrived at the palace and, in case he had any ideas to the contrary, her door was securely locked.

Theirs was a paper marriage so he could grab the throne he coveted. She'd played her part for her sister's sake and to secure peace if she could. The last thing her beloved Jeirut needed was civil strife while the Emir of Halarq was threatening them, which official sources had confirmed he really was. Huseyn hadn't lied about that.

Ghizlan yanked out an ancient oversized T-shirt that was anything but seductive. True, she hadn't worn it since studying abroad. True, it was a defiant act no one but she would know about. But the thought of wearing that provocative nightgown sent a chill through her that wasn't about being cold, but an inner heat she didn't want to acknowledge.

Because it led inevitably to images her wired brain supplied too easily. Of Huseyn stripping the ruby lace straps off her shoulders with those big callused palms and kissing his way down to—

'No!' She slammed the drawer and stomped into the bathroom. She refused to think about Huseyn al Rasheed in that way. It was a betrayal of her self-respect. He'd forced her into marriage. He wasn't forcing her into anything else.

No matter how her rebellious body responded to his masculinity. She wasn't *that* masochistic!

A whole afternoon and evening in his company had been more than enough. Yet as she unpinned her hair, unfastened the jewels and put them in their cases, then slipped out of her dress, her thoughts turned to him time and again.

To her annoyance and unwilling admiration, he'd been perfectly at home hosting their formal wedding banquet. Arcane court etiquette and even the ridiculously large choice of cutlery for the multi-course meal hadn't fazed him. Obviously his province wasn't as rustic as she'd supposed. He'd proven a fine host, attentive and urbane. He'd even had the grace to allow Azim, fretful and apologetic, time alone with her. She'd found herself lying to the distressed old man, telling him she was okay, that the marriage was her choice.

Ghizlan finished cleansing her face and splashed cold water over her cheeks. She *wasn't* okay. Not one man amongst those present had made a move to question the marriage or stand up for her rights. Far easier to accede to the fiction she'd chosen to marry a brute intent on seizing personal power.

Except he didn't seem...

No. She wasn't going there. Huseyn presented the persona he knew others wanted to see. As for her unwanted response to that ultra-masculine vibe of his—she'd squash it eventually. All she had to do was concentrate on how loathsome he was.

Her response wasn't really about *him*, but *her*. It was high time she found herself a man. As soon as the divorce came through and she had the freedom to act for herself instead of as a royal princess, always under press scrutiny, that's what she'd do. She'd find a man who attracted and respected her. One she could imagine herself caring for.

She picked up her toothbrush and scrubbed her teeth vigorously.

Despite her exhaustion she was wired. Today's events had awakened such intense emotions, not least indignation, and she was ashamed to say—fear, that she knew she wouldn't sleep any time soon.

Ghizlan turned to the door and raised her hand to the light switch. She didn't feel like reading. She'd turn on her computer and—

'What are you doing here?' Her eyes bulged as she took in the tall form lounging against the bedroom wall, one long finger stirring the diamond glitter of the bracelet she'd discarded on the dressing table. Sparks of light flashed at his touch. Matching sparks ignited her temper and something else, hot and shivery, deep inside.

Her hackles rose. 'How did you get in?' Her gaze snapped to her door, securely shut.

Huseyn shrugged, surveying her from under hooded eyes. 'With a key, of course.' That deep voice was pitched even lower than usual, running like a stream of velvet right through her middle.

Ghizlan bit her lip. Of course he had a key. He'd taken over the Palace of the Winds. It had only been a fiction these last few days that she and Mina had any real privacy in their own home. The realisation smacked her hard in the chest.

She stiffened, torn between the desire to eject him and to cover herself up. Except for the mortifying, infuriating knowledge she could no more force this giant lump of a man to move than she could the Palace itself. And her wrap was in her wardrobe. Besides, her huge T-shirt covered her from neck almost to knee.

Show no fear. Once she showed trepidation he'd have the advantage.

As if he doesn't already have that!

Ghizlan's hands tightened on the velvet jewellery boxes

as she walked towards him, keeping her eyes on his face, not the shadow of dark hair she thought she saw through the fine weave of his open-necked shirt.

Wordlessly she scooped up the bracelet and placed it in its box then shut the lid. She needed to put the jewellery boxes down but that meant she'd have nothing to hide behind and the keen way those silver-blue eyes surveyed her, she wasn't ready to do that.

'You're not Sheikh yet.' The words emerged from between clenched teeth. 'And even if you were, you have no right in my room.'

Balancing the jewellery cases on one arm, she held out her other hand. 'I'll take that key. Whatever you want to discuss can wait till tomorrow. I've played my part in your little farce.' Ghizlan paused, swallowing to banish the wobble in her voice. 'Now I'd like to go to bed.'

'At last,' he murmured. 'Something we agree on.' Before she could stop him he reached out and plucked the boxes from her, placing them on the dresser.

Instantly the air around her sucked tight as if he'd somehow stolen the oxygen she needed.

Her hands fell to her sides as she fought the urge to cover herself as his gaze skated lower, taking in her bare legs and feet, then up to the bulky white shirt she hoped to heaven covered her adequately. Except, even as she assured herself it did, her breasts tightened, tingled, and her nipples puckered.

Abruptly she crossed her arms, high and tight, over heaving breasts. 'Get. Out. Of. My. Room.'

She'd never looked more stunning. In diamonds and velvet she'd been regal and sexily sophisticated. In the trousers and black top she'd worn to scale the castle walls she'd been vulnerable and outrageously provocative.

In a T-shirt that skimmed those amazing curves and gave him his first uninterrupted view of her long, long legs, she was the most voluptuous, alluring woman he'd ever known. His heart hammered his ribs as anticipation welled.

She wasn't even trying to seduce. He guessed she didn't realise how the bathroom light behind her revealed so much she tried to hide. And that spark of hauteur in her eyes, the sulky turn-down of her plush lips...

Huseyn dragged in much-needed air through his nostrils, registering the rich cinnamon-honey scent he'd become addicted to since meeting Ghizlan.

'This is *our* room, my lady.'

As expected, she drew herself up, bristling. He loved her spunk. The way she came out of her corner fighting every time.

'Oh, no.' She backed a step, shaking her head. 'Don't think it even for a minute. That was never part of the agreement.'

Huseyn folded his arms rather than reach for her and tug her to him. 'You agreed to marry me. And now, as my wife, you're—'

'Don't you *dare* preach to me about duty!' Those ripe breasts rose high and flame shot from his belly to his groin. 'I've done what you demanded because I was blackmailed into it. I will *not* be blackmailed into bed.'

Belatedly he raised his eyes to hers, seeing the flash of fury. Had he ever had a woman of such intense feelings? And the combination with her usual iron control made him wonder, as he'd wondered for days, what Princess Ghizlan would be like when she really let herself go. Adrenalin spiked in his blood.

'I have no intention of blackmailing you, *my lady.*' There was no sarcasm in his use of the word. Right now he revelled in the fact Ghizlan was exactly that, or soon would be. It had been that, as much as his concerns for the nation, interrupting his sleep for days.

'Good, then you can get out now.'

Huseyn took a single step, blocking her exit. 'I'm spending the night with my wife.'

She shook her head, luxurious ebony tresses coiling over her shoulders and sliding around her breasts. Huseyn's mouth dried and he swallowed. His need for her was so urgent. He had to rein it in.

'That's not going to happen, Huseyn.' Stupid to enjoy the sound of his name on her tongue. But he was so hungry for her even that was like a flurry of rain on parched, desert soil, accepted greedily. 'Unless you intend to use force.'

Her eyelids flickered and for a horrible moment he thought he read fear. For a moment only, until her body reassured him. Her nipples thrust needily towards him over those fiercely crossed arms. Neither did he miss the subtle perfume she exuded. Her usual sweet fragrance had altered to the light musky note of female arousal.

Fierce elation gripped him. A smile tugged one taut cheek. 'We both know there's no need for force. You want me, Ghizlan, and I want you. It was there when you kissed me—'

'I didn't kiss you!' She shifted away, but found herself backed against the wall. 'You forced yourself on me.'

'And you kissed me back with an enthusiasm that bodes very well for our sexual relationship.'

She was swinging her head from side to side in emphatic denial. 'The only way you'll get sex from me is rape.' She drew herself up to her full height, the fire in her eyes lighting a blaze in his belly.

He stepped forward. 'You know that's not—'

Only nimble reflexes saved him from the massive glass paperweight she shot at his face. Huseyn tossed it over his shoulder to bounce on the floor.

A hairbrush came next. He batted it aside.

Then an antique clock that he caught and placed on the far end of the dressing table, out of her reach.

The marble-framed photo came next, nearly clipping his

ear, making him surge forward to snap his hands around her wrists.

'Enough!'

She was trembling all over, the pulse at her wrist galloping. Huseyn breathed deeply, inhaling the intoxicating scent of her. 'Stop fighting me. You know it's pointless.'

'Because you're strong enough to take me even though I despise you?' She spat the words, her eyes bright, her pale golden skin flushed. Even now she fought what they both felt.

Slowly he shook his head, his eyes never leaving hers. Whatever this connection was between them, he'd never known its like. Never had a woman mesmerised him so. It was clear she felt it too, no matter how she fought it.

He captured both her wrists in one hand and lifted the other to her cheek. She gulped, the movement emphasising the slender, perfect line of her throat. Since when had a woman's throat been so enticing? Her eyelids fluttered as he stroked his knuckle over downy soft flesh. Heat rose to meet him. A tremor jerked through him at the delicacy of her skin. Like a rose petal, far too fragile for the touch of a rough hand like his.

Then she exhaled. A silent, fluttery sigh and her head tilted into his touch. Just for a millisecond. Until she realised what she was doing and jerked away.

'I don't want you. I'd never want a brute like you.'

'Liar,' he murmured, watching her swallow again.

'You come in here, you *force* yourself on me and you accuse me of *lying*!' She looked down. 'What are you doing?'

'Letting you go. You know I won't hurt you.' He opened his fingers, releasing her wrists, repressing a shudder of need as her hands slipped from his. He was strung so tightly it was a wonder he had the patience for these games. But he had to be sure. 'You're free to walk away.' He paused. 'As soon as I get a goodnight kiss from my wife.'

Shining dark eyes, huge and outraged, stared up into his. 'But I—'

The rest of her words were muffled as he bent and kissed her. Not hard, not fiercely, but with a slow, sure sense of rightness that nevertheless blasted the back of his skull like a blow from flying shrapnel.

He'd waited so long—days—since he'd tasted her. And it was as well he had, because falling into the lush softness of those open lips, the world splintered, falling away as he lost himself in her sweetness.

Everything—the sheikhdom, tonight's diplomatic negotiations under cover of their wedding banquet, even the threat from Halarq—receded to nothing when he tasted Ghizlan.

Manfully he kept his hands at his sides, allowing her the freedom to break the kiss, knowing in the marrow of his bones that she wouldn't. How could she resist the powerful attraction that had sparked between them from the very first moment?

Even so, tension ratcheted up as seconds passed and she stood, stoic and unresponsive. As his own need battered at the confines of his self-imposed restraint.

Then, finally, with a sound that might have been a groan or a sob, her lips moved tentatively against his and her eyes closed. Sensation exploded as her tongue tangled with his and she tilted her head, allowing him further in.

With one arm he hauled her to him, up on her toes, so she pressed her whole length against him, cradling him with those gorgeous hips, her belly cushioning his swollen length and her breasts...

He cupped her jaw, angling her face to his, diving into a kiss that sent every sense into overdrive.

She had to stop. She had to force him away.

She had to dredge up her sense, even if it was too late to salvage her pride.

Urgent commands raced through her brain. Rational, logical commands to assert herself and shove him away. Yet Ghizlan couldn't find the strength to obey.

Not when his mouth fused with hers in a kiss that should have been rapacious but instead was lushly inviting, slow yet demanding in a way that shattered all her preconceived notions of what a kiss could be. Even that earlier kiss in her father's study hadn't prepared her for the sheer need that welled within her as Huseyn made love to her mouth with his.

For that's what this was. He didn't plunder, he pleasured. He didn't demand, he invited, tempted, *lured* her into abandoning a lifetime's caution, so sweetly that her blood sang and her defences disintegrated.

It must be the recent trauma, the tension of the last days, a prisoner forced time and again to confront a man who should, on every account, disgust her yet who instead fascinated her. She hated the way he used her to further his ambition, despised his tactics, yet found herself drawn to him, her blood fizzing with an excitement that scandalised, scared and excited.

With Huseyn she felt vibrant, alive and…sexy.

He urged her back to the wall, his solid frame pushing against hers from thigh to breast and her knees liquefied. Never had she been so close to a man. Never felt so delicate and feminine, responding to such flagrant maleness, quickening and softening against powerful hardness.

Ghizlan grabbed his shirt, revelling in the searing heat of his muscled chest, then slid her hands up to his shoulders, hanging on tight.

Maybe this was Stockholm syndrome, the bizarre fixation of a prisoner for her captor. But even as the thought trailed through her brain, it burnt to cinders as one big hand cupped her breast and her brain went into meltdown.

Nothing, ever, had felt so good. Quivers of ecstasy ran through her as his thumb pressed then circled and a betraying moan escaped her lips. That he swallowed the sound of it and responded with his own deep grunt of masculine pleasure only heightened Ghizlan's excitement.

That big, rough hand was so gentle, his touch so perfect, as if she'd waited all of her twenty-six years for this moment, this sensation. This man.

Runnels of fire traced down from her breast, down from her lips fused with his, down from her scalp where his long fingers massaged, to coalesce in a burning heat deep in her pelvis.

Ghizlan shifted, feeling the blatant weight of his erection high against her belly. To her shocked fascination she revelled in the promise of his aroused body.

She shouldn't be doing this. She should be ripping herself from his arms. But there was nowhere she wanted to be more than here, drawing in the almond and spice taste of Huseyn, revelling in all that powerful masculinity, the rock-hard muscle taut against her softer frame. The combination of desire and curiosity was irresistible.

Shuddery ripples of delight rayed from his touch as he caressed her breast and her hair and Ghizlan all but purred.

Never had she ignored responsibility or propriety. Both had been drummed into her since childhood. Letting all that go in a blast of unadulterated sexual hunger was the most intoxicating experience of her life.

Ghizlan lifted onto her toes, slipped her hands inside Huseyn's collar and welded her fingers against the satiny heat of his shoulders, answering his deep, potent kiss with demands of her own.

Seconds later his hands slid around her thighs, lifting her high then pressing her back against the wall, his pelvis hard against hers.

Astounded at how *right* that felt, Ghizlan's eyes popped open to meet his hooded, silvery stare. His mouth lifted from hers, just enough for them to gasp for air, their chests rising together, making her sensitised breasts tingle needily.

Now was the time to demand he let her go. To grab control.

But it wasn't control she needed. It was this man who'd torn away her blinkers and made her feel things she'd never understood existed.

There'd be hell to pay later. Sex wouldn't remove the vast chasm between them. But to turn back now, to retreat into the safety of duty and dignity, was impossible. Ghizlan had fought him with everything she had but now she needed him with every nerve and sinew and muscle and bone in her body. Even her brain craved him.

She should cringe away and beg for a reprieve but she wasn't that much of a coward. Those slumberous pale eyes promised pleasure. So did those deft hands and the sensual mouth that had so thoroughly seduced her.

For once in her life she was going to have what *she* wanted, not what duty dictated, and damn the consequences.

So when he lifted her thigh over his hip, tucking her calf around him, Ghizlan let him. Let him position her other leg too, so she was wound around him, ankles locked at his back. His erection was solid and provocative against her feminine core and it was all she could do not to squirm closer. Her breaths were short, out of control, and her pulse throbbed erratically.

The sight of Huseyn's pulse flickering just as fast at the base of his throat proved this was mutual. She wanted to taste him there, where the sheen of heat burnished his dark gold skin.

'Ghizlan.' He stretched the word out, like the sigh of the wind swirling round the battlements. Or maybe that was her own sigh as he folded one arm around her, drawing her close so her breasts crushed against his broad chest. The glitter in his eyes held a promise she yearned to accept.

When his mouth came down on hers it was hard, almost punishing, yet she revelled in his hunger, meeting it with her own, gripping him tightly with her legs, her hands clamped on his shoulders. She lost herself in it, only vaguely aware of movement till they toppled, her over him, onto the bed.

Limbs tangled, her cheek scraped his hard jaw and her fingers dug hard into his flesh. There was a waft of cooler air as he reefed her T-shirt off, forcing her to let go of him so he could drag it over her head and away. Then flurried movements as he discarded his clothes and came back to her, his super-heated flesh smooth in places, in others tickling with the abrasion of hair, a brand new, wondrous territory to explore.

Ghizlan slid her instep over his calf, fascinated at the texture of coarse hair and solid muscle. Her hand cupped his biceps then slid to his shoulder, silky smooth and broad. Her other hand pressed at the curve of his chest where his heart pounded, then inched down his torso, following the tantalising trail of narrowing hair she'd seen so briefly as he'd hauled off his shirt.

'Later,' he growled, capturing her hand in his.

That searing light gaze held hers and something shot through her. Something she had no name for, but felt right to the centre of her being. Shared purpose. Understanding. Something so elemental and real it was hard to believe they were virtual strangers.

Her husband—the man she barely knew.

But as he tugged her other hand up to his shoulder, at the same time lowering his body to lie within the curve of her hips, as she felt the weight of him where no man had ever lain, it didn't feel as if they were strangers. It was better than she could have imagined.

Her mind overloaded on sensation. His breath, steamy on her lips. His hip bones, hard against her. His erection thick and impossibly long, pressing against her belly. The intimate fragrance of their hot flesh together. The friction when he slid lower.

'Easy.' Huseyn's voice sounded clogged. He kissed her when she jerked and trembled at the powerful sensations unleashed as his body aligned against hers. As he took possession of her mouth she melted again, caught up in delicious abandonment. And when he slid down her body, cupping her breast, licking it, circling her nipple with his tongue, then finally drawing the sensitised peak into his mouth and drawing hard—

Ghizlan dug her fingers into him, her back arching and a sob tearing from her mouth. So good. Who'd have guessed it would feel so good? So—

His teeth closed around her nipple with a little tug and an incendiary dart shot straight to her womb. He did it again and she heard a sharp, keening cry as pleasure ripped through her. Once more she arched against him, fingers in his hair, dragging him closer, and still it wasn't enough.

Pleasure came in waves with each suck and nip of his mouth at his breast. Then, through the haze, she felt the slide of long fingers against her body, right down to her entrance, curling in to where she was slick and hot.

'So eager.' His voice was gravel and velvet, honeyed yet rough, and it tore at something in her. He kissed her hard, his tongue delving deep. 'I need you, Ghizlan.'

Of its own volition her body clamped his fingers, shocking her. This was glorious but so fast, so far beyond what she knew. 'I'm not—'

But Huseyn was kissing her again. Hard, demanding kisses that stifled her half-formed protest. Words spiralled away, her doubt lost as her body quickened.

He stroked her deftly, lingeringly, and fire flickered in her blood.

'Tell me you want this.' His deep voice burred through her. She felt hollow inside, achy and restless. She'd never felt— 'Ghizlan?'

'Yes,' she gasped. *Yes, yes, yes.* Her need for him pulsed with every beat of her heart. 'But I…'

He withdrew his hand and she couldn't stop a groan of dismay that he muffled with his lips. She craved him with an urgency unlike anything she'd experienced. Needily she tilted her hips.

She was holding him tight, kissing him back when he shifted. She felt the heat of his erection between her legs, then a surge of movement, impaling her, stretching her impossibly. Her eyes snapped open on a gasp of distress as pain ripped through her.

Diamond-bright eyes bored down into Ghizlan's as she froze, her breath choking in constricted lungs. She read heat and lust in his eyes and a glimmer of something that might have been surprise as he sank into her till they were locked tight.

For a frantic instant she panicked, believing she couldn't breathe.

He was hot, so hot, hard and unyielding. His huge body surrounded her, pushing her down into the bed despite the way he propped himself on his arms. His wide brow crunched in a ferocious frown and his breathing laboured as he held himself still. The weight of him inside her was so foreign she felt dazed.

Ghizlan's hands went to his shoulders as if to push him away and he withdrew, the slide of his body inside hers strange yet tantalising as pain ebbed.

She sucked in a shuddery breath, telling herself it was okay. That pain wasn't unexpected. It would be fine when she had time to adjust.

She stared into glittering eyes, reading regret there and in the twist of his lips. Then her breath stalled as Huseyn thrust again, his hips hard against hers as he surged long and deep, filling her.

'I'm sorry. I can't—' His words tore away.

Then his hand closed around her breast and excitement

jolted through her. She tried to catch it, hold it. A flicker of response trembled there, where his body joined hers. She dug her nails into the wide ridge of his shoulders, tentatively lifting her hips, instinctively seeking the friction that would intensify that fragile flutter of delight.

But with a sudden hoarse shout, Huseyn stiffened against her. The tendons in his neck stood proud, his eyes closed in a wince of concentration and his body arched, pinioning her to the mattress as the heavy pulse of his orgasm filled her.

Despite the dull echo of pain just turning into pleasure, Ghizlan was fascinated by the sight of him, so big and powerful, lost in the moment of ecstasy. Within her the rhythm of his rapture continued and she shifted as arousal surged anew.

But it was too late. Huseyn was drawing away.

To her surprise, Ghizlan regretted the moment when they separated, feeling something almost like loss. She wanted to hold him to her, cuddle him and feel the slowing beat of his heart. She wanted to feel again that beat of arousal and experience her own climax when they were joined.

But instead of gathering her close, or lying, lost in satiation, Huseyn rolled away. He sat for a moment on the side of the bed, shoulders bowed and hands braced on the mattress. Then abruptly he pushed to his feet and strode to the bathroom.

Ghizlan stared, hating the way her gaze trawled the dark gold skin of his back, the delicious, tight curves of his buttocks, and his easy, comfortable-in-his-body gait.

Even when he entered the other room and flicked on a light she waited, telling herself he'd turn and speak, say something.

He shut the door between them without turning. It snicked closed with a finality that lodged a weight in her chest.

Her body throbbed, but not from completion. Her legs were wobbly and suddenly she was close to tears.

What had she expected? Tenderness? A union of souls?

She flopped back and stared at the high ceiling. There'd been tenderness, at least until he'd got her where he wanted her. But after that? Her brain clung to the moment of apology. *I'm sorry. I can't.* Can't what? Can't stop? Can't give you what you want?

Huseyn was the experienced one. The one who'd bragged about satisfying his lovers. Despite her discomfort she'd felt excitement at his possession and something like awe as he'd climaxed within her. She'd felt the slow bubbling of rapture. But then he'd simply turned away and ignored her.

Ghizlan swallowed, blinking back stupid, hot tears. Had that really been too much to expect? Had she been so wrong, believing they shared a mutual passion?

Of course she was wrong. He'd wed her and bedded her for one reason only—to get power. He wasn't interested in anything else, including a wife who didn't even have the conviction to push him away when he hauled her into his arms.

She'd betrayed herself. She'd given in when she should have fought.

She'd succumbed.

Setting her jaw tight, Ghizlan rolled over and stared at the closed bathroom door. Self-loathing threatened to swamp her but she shoved it aside and focused on determination instead.

Huseyn had played her for the last time.

CHAPTER EIGHT

HUSEYN TURNED THE TAP to full, letting the cold water pound him, hard and needle-sharp. Yet each tiny stab from each streaming shower jet only made him more aware of his body than before, not less. The needling discomfort was nothing to the disgust channelling through his gut, leaving a gaping hollow where his self-respect used to reside.

He sluiced water from his face then propped his palm against the tiled wall, leaning hard as his body sagged.

He shook his head, still horrified at what he'd done. Taken Ghizlan—beautiful, defiant, wary Ghizlan—with the finesse of a rutting ram.

Even when he'd realised she was a virgin, had he stopped? Had he pulled back and made her first time easier?

Huseyn's eyes squeezed shut at the memory of how he'd been unable to restrain himself, so lost in thrall to her glorious body and the drugging hunger that overrode his brain and left his libido in control of his body.

The dazed shock in her beautiful eyes had shot an arrow straight to his conscience. He'd known he had to pull away, but for the first time ever, intending and doing had been two separate things. He hadn't been able to do more than begin to apologise, because he'd been overtaken by the most intense, all-consuming climax of his life.

He dragged a hand over his face, almost surprised to feel familiar features. He felt as if he was no longer the man he'd been. What he'd done—hurting Ghizlan—went against every code of honour. His pride revolted.

He'd brushed off her jibes about him taking unwilling women, about him possibly hurting lovers because of his size, because of course it was nonsense. Aware of his greater bulk, Huseyn always held back, ensuring his lover's pleasure and never letting go completely. Now, unbelievably, he'd done as she'd accused and he didn't know what to do with himself. His skin was too tight and his conscience too big.

Wrenching off the taps, he reached for a towel and began to dry himself.

He couldn't have expected her to be a virgin at her age. Surely not. And she'd spent years in the West, supposedly studying, but, he'd assumed, partying and living a life of idle pleasure.

How could she have been a virgin?

How could a woman who looked like that have reached her mid-twenties and not—?

He was making excuses. As soon as he'd discovered she was a virgin he'd had a duty to withdraw, to soothe and ease her into sex.

Instead he'd succumbed to selfishness. Absorbed in the rapture of Ghizlan's capitulation, he hadn't been able to put the brakes on. He'd lost himself in mere seconds.

There'd been a heady elation in taking his wife's untried body. In the sudden, overwhelming knowledge that he was her first and only lover. It had shattered his control even as he'd ordered himself to stop.

No wonder he hadn't been able to face her afterwards. He could imagine the reproach in those dark velvet eyes. For once her estimation of him had been right. And for the first time in his life he'd run, unable to look her in the face while guilt devoured him.

Huseyn stiffened. Perhaps she was still in pain. What could he do to ease that?

Hell! He knew nothing of virgins, had carefully avoided them. Until now.

He'd go back and take her in his arms, show her the tenderness she deserved. Then he'd give her orgasm after orgasm to make up for the disaster of their first coupling. He'd deny himself all night if he had to, for fear of hurting her again. He'd be gentle. He'd ease her into ecstasy, erasing the memory of what had gone before. Though he knew he couldn't eradicate his shame any time soon.

He reached for the trousers he'd grabbed on the way to the bathroom and dragged them on. One final scrub of his wet hair with a towel, then he was striding to the door. He should have stayed with her, should have—

'What are you doing?' He slammed to a stop in the doorway. From across the room dark eyes met his and he felt the jolt of response right to the bare soles of his feet.

Far from lying, curled in a ball of misery and pain, Ghizlan was on her feet, covered once more by that long white T-shirt that did virtually nothing to hide her luscious body. Huseyn's blood quickened, his groin grew tight as she moved and her beautiful breasts swayed against the fabric, pebbled nipples visible even from here.

Damn it. He should have stayed under the cold water longer. It had done nothing to combat his arousal.

'Ghizlan?' Still she didn't answer, but tugged at the bedding. Already the pillows and bedspread lay tossed on the floor.

He strode towards her, saw her sidelong glance and the way her jaw tightened, and stopped on the other side of the bed.

'What are you doing?' He planted his hands on his hips, welding them there before he was tempted to reach for her. Her hair was a dark, glossy cloud that screamed an invitation for his touch. Her mouth, turned down in a sulky pout, would taste like heaven, he knew. And those legs. The feel of them wrapped around his waist had driven him beyond thought. He locked his jaw and drew on all his willpower to keep his distance. He needed to be calm, gentle, reassuring.

She wrenched the bedsheet free from one corner and

hauled it towards her. That was when he saw the dark stain on its centre. Fresh blood. Ghizlan's blood.

Huseyn stumbled forward half a step before he found his balance. An invisible fist had smacked him in the solar plexus. Another hand chopped the back of his knees, loosening his stance.

He drew a deep breath, telling himself it was a small stain after all, and inevitable. That if it hadn't been him it would have been someone else taking her virginity. But rationalisations didn't work. Not when he felt marrow-deep guilt over hurting her.

But what really fuelled his guilt was that it wasn't just regret he experienced. Reliving those moments when he'd possessed her in that most elemental way excited him.

He wanted her again. Right now.

'What do you think I'm doing?' She didn't bother to look at him. He wondered if the sight of him so disgusted her she couldn't bring herself to meet his eyes.

The sheet tugged free and she hauled it into her arms, turning away not towards the door but the window.

'Talk to me, Ghizlan.'

Now there was a first, asking a woman to talk. But this was different. *She* was different.

One-handed she wrenched aside the curtain and wrestled with the window catch. 'What do you think I'm doing?' She paused and shot a look of pure loathing over her shoulder. 'Hanging the sheet from the window so all of Jeirut can see our marriage has been consummated. The Royal Council will want proof I've been appropriately deflowered and—'

'Stop it!'

It was only as the sound echoed around the room that Huseyn realised he'd roared the order. That stain was proof he'd acted like a savage. He couldn't look at it.

He swallowed hard, banishing emotion, searching for calm. He hadn't even realised he'd moved until his hand closed around Ghizlan's shoulder. She shrank back as if his touch burnt.

Horrified, Huseyn dropped his hand. Her breasts rose and fell with each sharp breath. Her face was hectically flushed, her lips twisted in pain or fury and this close her eyes looked febrile. It struck him that finally he'd broken through Ghizlan's unbreachable control.

But it wasn't triumph Huseyn felt in the coiling, burning pit of his conscience. Watching her reaction, he felt like the barbarian she'd branded him. So much for being a man of honour.

Through everything she'd maintained a proud air of invincibility, even when the odds had been stacked against her. But here in this room, he'd shattered that. He hoped he hadn't destroyed it completely. Her pride and her determination to stand up to him were, he realised, part of what attracted him.

As if she wants to attract you.

Judging by that glare, she'd like to boil you in oil.

'There's no need for that.' He kept his voice low and soothing.

'There's every need!' She fumbled with the latch, never taking her eyes off him. As if she expected him to lunge at her. That made his belly shrink in self-reproach. 'You don't leave anything to chance, do you? You couldn't wait to be made Sheikh the usual way—you had to marry a royal princess to cement your claim. Now it's time to prove you've done your *manly* duty and consummated the match.'

'Ghizlan.' He softened his voice and held out his hand. 'You don't need to do this.'

She shook her head so wildly her hair swung wide, streaming across his outstretched hand.

'Why not?' Her voice was raw and bitter. 'That's all I am now. A means to an end. Not a person with hopes and plans and desires.' Her breath hitched. 'It's time to inform all your yes-men still down in the banqueting hall that you've—'

'Enough!' Huseyn wrenched the bunched sheet from her, lifting it out of her reach. He couldn't bear to hear any more. It shaved too close to the truth. He'd been so focused on the good of the nation he hadn't allowed himself to think about what this meant for Ghizlan. 'That's enough. You're becoming hysterical.'

'Hysterical?' The battle light in her eyes told him she'd cleave him in half if she could. Just as well there were no weapons in the royal apartments. 'It's typical of a brute like you to accuse a woman of being hysterical when—'

Huseyn had no plan other than to stop her tirade, hating the note, not just of anger but of despair, threading her voice. It made him sick to the core. So when she stepped in, reaching over his shoulder for the fine linen, he slammed his mouth down on hers. Anything to shut her up until he worked out how to calm her.

Except kissing Ghizlan had an inevitable effect on his still needy body. One touch of those lips, one taste and his other arm hooked round her, hauling her to him, soft breasts and belly cushioning his rigid frame.

He tried not to fall into the kiss. He tried to keep his head and think things through. But an instant later he was leaning in, delving deep, *willing* her to feel and respond to the same devil of desire that drove him.

His mouth gentled. He could coax her, he knew. Up until the moment he'd lost control Ghizlan had been with him all the way, kissing him with a fervour that had short-circuited his brain, wrapping those long legs around him as if she'd never let go. He deepened the kiss to a languorous caress he knew would seduce. He'd—

The sudden tang of salt on his tongue pierced his thoughts.

'No!' With a violent shove, Ghizlan thrust him off, the

heels of her hands digging into his chest. He rocked back, blinking as she stepped away. 'Get off. I don't want this!'

Over-bright eyes stared up at him.

Stunned, he saw the track of a tear down one pale cheek. It belied her fighting stance, hands on hips and feet planted wide. And it made his heart lurch in his chest.

Her mouth was swollen from his passion and there was a mark on her neck where he must have nipped her with his teeth. He couldn't remember doing it.

Is that going to be another of your excuses?

I didn't know she was an innocent.

I don't remember hurting her.

Hell! He stepped back, bile rising. How close had he come to losing control again?

Huseyn backed away another step. Always, even as a skinny, underfed kid, he'd understood what he had to do. Help his mother scrape a living in their dirt-poor village. Then, when she died, find the father who'd abandoned them. Later it had been to do everything it took to become a warrior. Not simply any warrior but the best in the province, so good his father would finally have to acknowledge him, however grudgingly. Always he'd believed he'd acted honourably. Given his father's appalling example, Huseyn took pride in doing the decent thing always. Until now.

Shame scythed through him, slicing at his self-respect. With this one woman, he'd behaved anything but honourably.

Yet even now, staring into her beautiful drowned eyes, reading the defiant tilt of her chin and the distress turning her breathing into staccato gasps, he hungered for her. The desire, no, the *need* to possess her, hummed through him like wind through a desolate mountain canyon. As desolate as his soul.

He couldn't stay here. He didn't trust himself. He swung on his heel and marched to the door, determined to have himself under control before he faced his wife again.

* * *

Ghizlan stared, blinking, at her husband's unreadable face.

He felt something, she knew he did from the way his mighty chest rose with each deep breath. And the way tiny lines bracketed his mouth and his nostrils flared. But his eyes gave nothing away.

Or maybe the problem was her—she was so lost to the myriad sensations he'd awoken—*again*—with that kiss, she was too befuddled to do more than gawk.

The man only had to kiss her and she lost it!

Even with that dull ache gently throbbing between her legs and disappointment vying with fury for pre-eminence, her one, overwhelming response when he touched her was to lean in and let him do exactly what he wanted.

It was bizarre. But when he'd taken her mouth and pulled her to him, part of her, the largest part, had clamoured a triumphant *Yes!* She'd wanted to fall against him and let him seduce her all over again.

It was only the last, fragile remnants of pride that had saved her from responding.

That's why, to her horror, she'd cried. Because despite everything he'd done to her, despite the fact he was her enemy, using her person, her body, as a political tool, she'd come to crave him in a way that made a mockery of everything she'd ever believed about herself.

How low had she sunk?

She'd known he was dangerous, even if she'd never completely understood the exact nature of that lethal animal quality in his potent personality and rugged frame. But she understood now. The memory of that fleeting pleasure as he'd filled her body flashed through her, a devastating sense memory. She had to squeeze her eyes shut rather than look at his big, beautiful, loose-limbed frame.

She heard the door scrape and her eyes snapped open. She wanted to ask him where he was going. Whether he'd return. She wanted, foolishly, to reach for him.

Rigid, she kept her hands at her sides. 'What are you going to do with the sheet?' Her voice was tight and thin.

He paused but didn't turn. When finally he spoke she could tell it was through gritted teeth. 'Burn the damned thing.'

Then he was gone. Yet the image of him lingered—impossibly wide shoulders, acres of bare golden flesh over muscles that flexed and rippled with every movement, long, powerful legs and tousled dark hair. An erection that even now was as enticing as it was daunting.

Ghizlan was glad he'd gone. She never wanted to see him again. He'd turned her into a woman she despised—weak and needy, on the verge of promising anything to the enemy in the hope of physical pleasure.

She spun away and marched across the room, blinking back tears she'd never shed for her father.

In the bathroom she put the plug in the bath and wrenched the taps on. She locked the door. Surely he wouldn't interrupt her for a while. She had time to…what? Recover? Plan her opposition? Wish he'd made love to her again?

Distraught, she swung around and caught her reflection in the mirror. She didn't know whether to be pleased or worried that she hardly recognised herself.

CHAPTER NINE

'You're looking very regal today, my lady.'

Huseyn didn't utter his actual thought—that she was stunning. So gorgeous she'd made his heart kick as she crossed the vast audience chamber, the crowd parting before her. For an instant his breath had stilled.

'That's appropriate since I'm married to the man about to be proclaimed Sheikh.'

Her voice was cool, in stark contrast to the fiery termagant who'd ripped the sheet off their bed last night, and the lover who'd melted against him as he'd kissed her, her soft mews of pleasure driving him crazy.

Totally unlike the woman whose drowning eyes had driven him from her room, not to return.

The well of self-disgust he'd tapped into last night surged high. Had he done right, leaving her alone? At the time it had seemed the only sensible course.

Not by so much as a quiver did she display that her thoughts strayed to their disastrous wedding night. Instead a casual hand gesture dismissed both him and the treasures she wore: a gold and ruby necklace and a delicate ruby-studded diadem, rich against her ebony hair.

Huseyn surveyed her from the crown of her intricate hairstyle to her satin high heels. He particularly enjoyed the long, square-necked dress she wore—simple yet devastatingly feminine.

He'd never paid attention to women's clothes, except for the mechanics of removing them. With Ghizlan that changed.

His gaze followed the dip and swell of her small waist and rounded hips with a lover's appreciation, the smooth line of her long thighs. The dark red suited her.

Blood red, it was.

A deliberate reminder of last night's disastrous bedding. A warning she remembered exactly why he'd married her and that she refused to give in to him. Marginally more subtle than wearing mourning to yesterday's wedding. This message was for him alone, a private challenge.

Relief filled him. She wasn't broken after all, despite what his conscience had said whenever he recalled her pain last night.

Huseyn's eyes rose swiftly, catching her off guard.

That's when he saw it, the shadow in her gaze, the distress in her too-tight mouth. Proof that despite her brave show, Ghizlan was hurting. Scared? The notion cut like a blade.

'Ghizlan, we need to talk. About last night—'

Her eyes widened and she shook her head. 'There's nothing to say.'

Nothing to say? Then he saw her gaze flick to the crowd of guests. They were far enough away not to overhear but still...

'Very well. We'll discuss it after the ceremony.'

'I'm afraid that won't be possible.' Distress was replaced by hauteur as she angled her chin. Her eyes sparkled and her nostrils thinned in regal disapproval. 'I have some longstanding commitments later. I've already had to cancel appointments to attend this...' her mouth flattened '...ceremony.'

So that's how she was going to play it.

Huseyn knew what she was doing. Masking feelings with a show of unconcern. How often as a kid had he pretended nonchalance when petrified by fear?

Disdain was easier for Ghizlan than bridging the gulf between them. Who could blame her?

Besides, the international situation was so fraught that *had* to be his priority. There'd be time later to fix the damage he'd done last night.

Meanwhile, let her play the disdainful aristocrat. He could weather her scorn. She had no way of knowing her defiance attracted rather than repelled him.

'Let me congratulate you,' he murmured. 'You look every inch the royal consort. The colour suits you.'

Her expression didn't alter but the wash of heat up her throat told him what words couldn't.

'Thank you, my lord. So do you. Very…impressive.' She made a production of scanning him, from his traditional headscarf to the toes of his crimson kid boots, pausing a fraction too long on the ceremonial dagger at his side. 'The broadcast of today's ceremony will be a national sensation since you're the star.'

By all that was sacred, this woman was superb. She stood there proud and serene, a perfect smile on those perfect lips, as if she hadn't a worry in the world. As if calling him her lord wasn't like swallowing bitter aloes.

This was the sort of woman he needed beside him. A woman who wasn't afraid to—

Huseyn stilled. He was a loner and always had been. Their marriage was a necessity forced by circumstance. Yet he found himself enjoying the prospect of getting to know his wife, and not just sexually.

'Is there a problem, *my lord*?'

She was quick. No one else read him so easily.

'None at all.' He reached out and gripped her elbow, feeling the tiny quiver of reaction she couldn't hide.

Her eyes met his, rounding slightly. Once more Huseyn considered broaching last night's debacle. But she wasn't ready. He sensed it was only outrage giving Ghizlan courage to continue. *That* he could accommodate.

He inclined his head, invading her space. 'You can still feel it, can't you, *my lady*? You didn't really think what's between us is so easily destroyed?'

Her nostrils flared as if inhaling an offensive odour.

'On the contrary, I know only too well how binding our marriage is. Until you choose to dissolve it.'

He moved to one side, his mouth against her ear. 'Are you already counting the days? I find the idea of you impatiently waiting for me quite endearing.'

Ghizlan turned her head to stare up at him, eyes dark and fathomless as an abandoned desert well, and he knew exactly how treacherous those could be for the unwary, desperate with thirst. She gave another perfect smile, this one showing even, white teeth and the beast in him, the beast he'd worked to leash since the moment he'd walked away from her bed, sprang to life with a growl of anticipation.

'The day you find me eagerly awaiting you is the day you know I've lost my mind. Which, now I consider, has some attraction as an alternative.'

Huseyn couldn't prevent a bark of laughter. She was priceless. Steely and determined. It was a pity she wasn't a man. She had more gumption than any of those present for today's ceremony.

Except Ghizlan as a man would be a crime against nature.

Last night it had taken more determination than he'd ever needed to walk away from her. He'd distracted himself by spending the rest of his wedding night locked with the nation's powerbrokers. They'd still been downstairs, celebrating his wedding, when he'd stalked in, determined that one thing at least would go as planned that night.

Ghizlan had been right. None of them had looked concerned that he'd left his bride's bed to wrangle over politics and press his case to become Sheikh. None save Azim who'd eyed him the way a sensible man watched a deadly asp.

It was good to know his wife had at least one champion in this throng of self-important men.

Why that mattered, Huseyn didn't know. Except he'd

be busy in the weeks to come trying to pull Jeirut from the brink of war. He didn't like to think of Ghizlan alone.

'Come. It's time.' He looped her hand through his elbow, clamping it with his hand—huge and scarred against her delicate fingers.

Theirs was an unlikely match. A refined princess and a lowborn soldier who knew more about hunger and hardship than banquets or ceremonies, despite his time as second in command and now as Sheikh in his province.

Yet he held her hand firmly as they crossed to the dais where the throne waited. He kept her at his side through the short, all-important ceremony, not because it was custom but because she deserved to be there.

That laugh. Who'd have thought it would make a difference?

But it had. The memory of it even now wound through Ghizlan like sweet syrup, hot and enticing, confusing her.

Who'd have thought Huseyn al Rasheed knew how to laugh? He specialised in glowering and stony-faced determination.

And raw passion. Remember?

Oh, she remembered too well. He was a big, burly brute but no matter how she rebelled at the idea, he had the uncanny ability to make her want as no man ever had. She was drawn to him by forces she'd never fully understood until he'd taken her in his arms, forces she'd blithely believed she could ignore with all the confidence of an untried innocent. Now she knew better.

But one thing hadn't altered. He was still her enemy.

Shame filled her and she set her jaw, trying to concentrate on her schedule for the day. She'd had eighteen days to practise nonchalance. Almost three weeks of Huseyn absent in the provinces, yet in regular contact with diplomatic advisers here in the capital. He'd left immediately after the ceremony that proclaimed him Sheikh and not once in that time had he contacted her.

Ghizlan closed her computer tablet and set it aside on the car's back seat. She turned to look out the window as the vehicle wound slowly through the oldest, poorest part of the city towards the outskirts.

Of course she hadn't expected a message from him. She heard enough from Azim in her daily briefings. She'd been torn between amazement and something almost like pride as she'd learned of Huseyn's success. Not through sabre-rattling or a pre-emptive military strike, but with canny diplomacy and a personal, if foolhardy show of courage.

He'd met the nephew of the ailing Emir of Halarq alone, without even a bodyguard, for hours of talks, in an isolated tent on the disputed border. What had passed there no one knew for sure but it had paved the way for officials to meet over the following weeks and painstakingly nut out an agreement between the two nations. Rumour had it that the Emir of Halarq was terminally ill and his nephew would succeed him soon. While relations weren't exactly friendly, there was solid hope for a longer term rapprochement.

That Huseyn had achieved that, the man who'd monstered and manipulated her, *used* her in ways that must appal any thinking woman, stunned her. Had she misjudged him as he'd misjudged her? Oh, he was still a self-satisfied macho, callous, cold-hearted beast, but he'd saved her beloved Jeirut and the fizz of relief in her veins was palpable.

But she was *not* on tenterhooks at the news he was returning today.

The car pulled to a halt and Ghizlan thrust aside unwanted thoughts of her unwanted husband. He'd done his job, saving the nation. She would do hers as she always had, patiently, painstakingly, even it if wasn't on a grand, international scale. It was still necessary and she was proud of what she and her people had achieved.

Huseyn rolled his shoulders against the padded seat and stretched his legs. He was weary after weeks of little sleep and the need to keep three steps ahead of the soon-to-be Emir of Halarq. The other man was ambitious and clever but not quite clever enough to best Huseyn, who'd won his knowledge of men and their weaknesses in a hard school.

The comfort of the limo, after the luxury of the longest, hottest shower he'd had time for in weeks, almost tempted him into closing his eyes. But it was only late afternoon. There was still much to do.

Like meet his wife.

He'd chosen to do that straight away. He'd spent only a few hours alone with her but the woman had got under his skin, like a thorn too deep to cut out. For weeks he'd thought of her at the oddest times, not only when he'd lain down to sleep and found himself recalling her soft body and the tiny sounds of pleasure she'd made as he'd kissed her into oblivion.

He looked around with interest as the car passed the ragged outskirts of the city. What was she doing out *here*? Azim had spoken of her busy schedule and Huseyn had imagined lunch with ambassadors' wives at upmarket restaurants. Or a goodwill visit to a hospital or charity.

They drew up in an isolated spot, before a new building. Beyond it he glimpsed more buildings and a series of regular round ponds.

Huseyn stared. His wife was visiting a waste water treatment plant?

Not only visiting, he discovered when he made his way, unannounced, into the building, but talking knowledgeably. Huseyn paused in the doorway to what appeared to be a control room, listening to her engaged in a conversation that made little sense to him.

Clearly the woman he'd married was far more complex than he'd imagined. He'd underestimated her.

'Your Highness.' One of the men with Ghizlan bowed, drawing the attention of the cluster of people to Huseyn.

Slowly she turned from the computer and the display panels. She wore an elegant skirt and jacket the colour of dark mountain violets, which skimmed her gorgeous curves. Her eyes held his, totally expressionless. But he hadn't missed the almost imperceptible tightening of her shoulders, or the tiny turn-down of her mouth before she widened it into a polite smile.

A familiar spark ignited in his belly, confirming what he already knew—he'd been impatient to return to her.

Inexplicable. Impossible. But true.

Huseyn never wasted time hiding from the truth. He saved his strength for dealing with it.

'My lady.' He strode across the room and lifted her hand to his lips, breathing in her subtle sweet scent. He felt her hand shake, saw her mouth firm, and repressed a smile. She had no way of discerning the abrupt jolt of energy cleaving his insides as desire soared, and he had no intention of enlightening her. For now it was enough to know she felt it too.

'My lord.' She paused and he wondered if it was to choke back distaste. Yet she continued easily. 'Allow me to introduce everyone. First, the facility manager...'

What was he doing here? Why wasn't he neck deep in treaties and diplomatic wrangles, or bullying some poor hapless servant?

He looked big and bold and stole more than his share of oxygen, leaving her chest tight. He'd shaved and she saw with alarm the flicker of amusement in the long dimple cutting one lean cheek.

'I have a question.' That deep voice purred along her skin, making the fine hairs at her nape rise. She recalled the way it had resonated through her on their wedding night, making her feel things she'd never expected, never wanted to experience with a man like him.

'Yes?' Her voice was too sharp. She sucked in a calming breath.

'What's an anaerobic digester?'

He must have been listening for some time. That unsettled her. What did he want? Why had he come?

'Ah,' said the manager, 'we're very proud of that. It was the Sheikha's suggestion initially—'

'Really? Do tell.'

'Well, given our aim to maximise energy efficiency and Her Highness's special interest in the field—'

'Her special interest?' Huseyn turned to her, one eyebrow raised. Ridiculously she experienced a twinge of guilt, as if she'd been hiding some secret, when the truth was he'd never been interested enough to enquire.

'My degree,' she explained. 'I was one of the first Jeiruti women to study engineering.'

'And still the only female chemical engineer in the country,' the manager added proudly.

Huseyn's blue-grey eyes held hers and sensation kicked high in her chest. 'Quite an achievement,' he murmured. 'I didn't know chemical engineers specialised in waste water.'

'You'd be surprised,' she said. 'We work on all sorts of processes. Anything from power generation, mineral processing or water management to pharmaceuticals, biotechnology or manufacturing explosives.'

'Quite a lethal combination.' Huseyn's eyes didn't leave hers.

'Absolutely.' She let her teeth show when she smiled.

'And the digester?'

'It's working as well as we'd hoped,' said the eager manager. 'It breaks down organic waste to release a gas which we then use to produce electricity. This new plant is generating enough power to meet its own needs and contribute to the city's electricity grid.'

Instead of looking bored, Huseyn began asking questions, pertinent questions that showed a genuine interest. And so they went over it all again, explaining everything they'd already shown her.

Now he was here she was no more than a fly on the wall. Ghizlan swallowed her bitterness. It didn't matter. But the headache at the base of her skull had been building for hours and she'd love to sit. Her period had begun this morning and she felt rotten. Though at least it meant she wasn't pregnant! She couldn't bring a child into this disastrous marriage, which was why she planned to start the Pill tomorrow. Ghizlan was determined never to give herself to Huseyn again. And he'd shown his total lack of interest since their wedding night, but she'd take no chances.

She shifted, wishing she'd worn lower heels, when Huseyn's voice cut her thoughts.

'It's been fascinating, and a credit to you all. Thank you so much.' Then, with a series of swift farewells he was leading her outside where her driver held open the car door.

'Where's *your* vehicle?' She sank onto the seat, suppressing a sigh of relief.

'I sent it away. No point keeping two here when we can return together.'

The driver slid into the front seat. 'To the new factory, my lady?'

Ghizlan bit her lip. She still had just enough time for her planned visit, but with Huseyn beside her—

'That's right.' Huseyn spoke up.

'Surely you don't have time for this,' she murmured, glancing at the driver. 'It's your first day back in the capital. You must have plenty of other—'

'Nothing more important than seeing my dear wife.' At her fulminating stare his lips twitched into something verging on a smile. 'Unless you find my presence too distracting?'

Ghizlan didn't deign to answer. It was too close to the truth. The whole time he'd stood beside her at the water treatment plant she'd been a mass of nerves, unsettled because *he* was there.

Why had he come? What did he want?

Now she shut her eyes and leaned her head back, blocking him out. One more stop then back to her room for a warm shower and a cup of tea and something for the rising pain. All she had to do was put up with him a little longer.

'We're here.' The words tickled her ear. Or perhaps it was Huseyn's lips, soft and warm against her lobe. Ghizlan jerked awake and stared up into slate blue eyes that seemed to bore right down into her soul. She blinked and shuffled to one side, flesh prickling at his nearness as if she'd received a zap of electricity.

The trip could only have taken fifteen minutes. Could she really have fallen asleep with Huseyn beside her?

'And where, exactly, is here?' her husband asked as they stood, surveying the building before them.

A tickle of apprehension traced down Ghizlan's backbone but she ignored it. There was nothing to be nervous about. She just didn't like Huseyn peering into her life and her interests as if he had a right to. But now she was here she refused to turn away. This was important.

'A project of mine.'

'Yours, not the city's?'

She swung round to face him but that severely sculpted face was unreadable. No hint of sarcasm.

'It's a joint venture.' She was putting up the money with the bulk of her inheritance and the Council had supplied the site. 'It will link to some schemes that are already running—one to help aspiring businesswomen and another to provide employment for local women.'

'An all-female enterprise?'

Ghizlan shrugged, too fatigued to rise to the bait. 'If you read the statistics you'd know the bulk of the poor in Jeirut are women, as are the bulk of those without education or employment. This is one, small attempt to turn that around.'

She marched across the newly resurfaced pavement and into the building, not waiting to see if he followed. No doubt he'd view this project as insignificant when measured against his own recent efforts, but it mattered. Not just to her, but to the people whose lives it would change.

He caught up with her as she moved through the vestibule of the old building. His tread was silent, too silent for such a big man, but she knew he was there from the hum of awareness tickling her shoulder and back. It was as if he put out an electrical force that zapped when he got near.

'My lady. Your Highness.' The project manager, Afifa, bowed low and Ghizlan admired the other woman's unruffled demeanour. She was used to Ghizlan and they'd developed a good working relationship but Huseyn could be daunting.

Quickly Ghizlan introduced Afifa then paused, surprised when her husband didn't instantly take over. In fact, he seemed to be waiting for her to take the lead.

Ever-present suspicion rose.

'We're here for a progress check and update on the new extension to the building.'

He nodded, falling in step as she led the way. 'And this building is…?'

'It was used for distilling attar of roses, the essential oil for which Jeirut was famous. It fell into disrepair in the last few decades as demand dropped due to the availability of imported scent.' And because, as part of the country's modernisation, traditional endeavours, particularly those seen as cottage industries, were ditched in favour of new, large-scale enterprises.

She led the way through the old distillation room to the

vast space where once tonnes of rose petals were brought for processing. Even now Ghizlan fancied she inhaled an echo of that lush, intoxicating scent. She breathed deeply, feeling some of her tension ebb.

'You're expecting to restart production with flowers grown locally?' There was scepticism in his tone.

'Of course. We've been successfully cultivating roses since the Middle Ages, if not before. Plus there are native plants ideal for perfume making. Like the iris. You know it grows wild in the mountains? It thrives in arid, cold conditions. This region was once famous for myrrh and frankincense and—'

Ghizlan pulled up short, discomfited at her own enthusiasm. She'd forgotten she needed to keep him at arm's length. Instead she'd rambled about her pet project. He couldn't possibly be interested.

'So you'll make perfumes using only local ingredients. Traditional oils and such.'

When Ghizlan hesitated, Afifa smoothly filled the breach. 'There will be a range of traditional products, both for domestic consumption and, we hope, export. We plan to extend the irrigation at the base of the mountains to grow more raw ingredients ourselves. But as well...' Afifa smiled at Ghizlan '...the Sheikha plans to import ingredients from elsewhere. Cedar from Morocco, bergamot from the Mediterranean, jasmine, orange blossom and so on.'

'Our aim,' said Ghizlan, tilting her chin as she met her husband's unreadable eyes, 'is to establish a couture perfume industry to rival the biggest names in the business.' When he remained silent she continued, provoked. 'There's no reason why Jeirut shouldn't achieve what others have. We have experience in the field and a willingness to learn and innovate.'

'No reason at all,' he said finally. 'I applaud your ambition.' He turned to Afifa. 'So you've extended the building? In what way?'

Ghizlan's shoulders slumped. She hadn't realised she'd been holding her breath until it escaped in a soft sigh of relief.

Because she'd thought Huseyn would belittle the project? His opinion didn't matter. She hadn't let her father's doubts stop her. Yet as she followed Huseyn and Afifa into the new section of the building, still to be completed, she admitted she'd been tense, waiting for some offhand dismissal of this scheme that was so dear to her.

She pressed her palm to her stomach as it cramped. That had to be the explanation. She was tired and vulnerable because of her hormones at this time of month. It couldn't possibly be because *his* approval mattered.

By the time they'd toured the new development, listened to Afifa's enthusiastic update on the business plan and progress on the irrigation programme, Ghizlan was all but swaying on her feet.

Thankful for the silent ride back to the palace, she nodded goodbye to Huseyn and headed to her room, only to find him shadowing her. She said nothing. No doubt he'd taken over the Sheikh's apartment, which lay in this direction.

But when she entered her apartment and found him following, brushing aside her arm when she would have shut the door, temper flared.

'You're not welcome in here!'

'Tell me something I don't know.' He had the audacity to lean back, propping one shoulder against the closed door and folding his arms across that powerful chest.

Something inside Ghizlan contracted, but not, she realised, in horror. It was more akin to excitement. Despite her now throbbing head and the pulling ache in her belly she found this man potently, inexplicably attractive.

Which made her angrier.

'This is my room and I don't want you here. Why don't you go back to wherever it is you've been sleeping?'

'From now on we sleep together, my lady. And I assume you'll be more comfortable here than moving into the royal quarters your father used.'

Seething, she turned her back on him then stopped short as she saw the view through the open door from her sitting room to her bedroom.

'What's happened to my bed?' It had been replaced with a massive, king-sized affair that cut off the oxygen supply to her lungs. If ever a bed screamed sex, this was it.

'I like to sprawl when I sleep.' That deep, rumbly voice rolled through her. 'And you must admit there's a lot of me. We'll be more comfortable this way.'

She swung back to glare at her tormentor. 'I have no intention of sleeping with you.'

The fire in his blue-grey eyes and the slow lift of one dark eyebrow were calculated to annoy. Ghizlan told herself she was angry. Not anxious about him or, worse, about her response to him.

'Or having sex!'

'That's a pity. I've been looking forward to that.' His eyes were pewter now, bordering on silver, and the sight of that sensual light sent a judder of response right to the soles of her feet.

'Because you enjoyed it so much? I don't care. You're not the lover I want.'

That snapped him to attention, all pretence at indolence gone. He stepped forward, crowding her.

'Who do you want, Ghizlan? Idris of Zahrat? The man who jilted you to marry someone else? Or maybe your Frenchman, Jean-Paul?'

Ghizlan stared up into eyes narrowed to gleaming slits. 'Don't be absurd.'

'I'm glad you realise it's absurd, *my lady*. Because the only man you're going to share yourself with is me.'

The way he loomed over her, his wide shoulders hemming her in, the tangy scent of him tantalising her nostrils, should have infuriated her. Yet Ghizlan found herself for a moment transfixed, a shudder of excitement ripping through her at his possessiveness.

Until she realised what she was doing and hauled herself away from him. 'We're not having sex.'

'Of course you don't want a repeat of our wedding night.' He followed her, step for step. 'For that I apologise. If I'd known in advance you were a virgin—'

'Stop!' She raised a hand. She didn't want to go there. Not even to ask what she'd ever done to make him assume she was anything but a virgin.

Living in the spotlight, she'd been cautious about dating. More than cautious, given her natural reticence about putting herself in any man's power. And when she'd lived overseas, studying, the paparazzi had always been waiting for a scoop about her, mingling with 'real' people. They'd approached her friends for tell-all exposés about the exotic, foreign princess. That had put Ghizlan off any inclination to pursue intimacy with a man, knowing the details would probably be splashed across the media.

'I. Don't. Want. Sex. With. You,' she said through clenched teeth. 'Got that?'

'Of course you do.' The nerve of the man left her speechless! 'But you're upset about our wedding night. It wasn't my finest hour but, believe me, I can do better.' His mouth kicked up at one corner and the gleam in his eyes burned so brightly it was like a spotlight, heating her where she stood. 'I promise you, Ghizlan, next time *will* be much better.'

Heat coursed through her, an insidious heat that trickled into places it shouldn't, making her wonder what it would be like if—

'There won't be a next time. Unless you intend to use force again.'

If he felt any remorse, he didn't show it. 'There was no force last time, just loss of control.' Hers or his, she wondered frantically as her breath caught. 'There *will* be a next time. But don't worry, I'll wait until you invite me.'

'Then you'll wait until hell freezes over.' She spun away from him but his callused hand caught hers. For reasons she couldn't fathom, she halted, looking down at the large, scarred hand that restrained her.

He wasn't taking no for an answer. He kept pushing her and pushing. But she had a trump card. One guaranteed to ward off any male.

'Let me go. I've got my period and I need the bathroom.'

As expected, he released her instantly. She strode to the sanctuary of her bathroom, wondering why her victory felt hollow.

CHAPTER TEN

HUSEYN WATCHED THE DOOR close behind her with a mixture of frustration and pride. Damn, but she was one feisty woman!

And hourly more intriguing.

His wife wasn't the pampered socialite he'd assumed. He recalled her conversation at the treatment works and the respect in which she was obviously held. Not just for her rank, but because she knew what she was talking about.

Then at the perfume factory. Her concern for the disadvantaged in their country was real. But instead of raising money the easy way through charity auctions or galas, she was building something concrete that would allow people the dignity of working towards a better life. She was magnificent, ideal for the role of royal consort.

He paced, fascinated by the barrage of insights into his wife. Not least was the passion in her. When she'd spoken of making perfume she'd lit up from within, as if she'd forgotten she spoke to *him*. That passion—he wanted it for himself. He wanted to obliterate the boundaries she'd put up, and the ones born of his clumsy treatment.

A grim smile curled his lips. She shouldn't be his priority. He still had to cement his rule over the nation. Plus there was a treaty with Halarq to finalise, not to mention one with Zahrat, which was precarious since Sheikh Idris had turned his back on Ghizlan.

A discordant note twanged through him at the thought of Idris. Obviously he and Ghizlan hadn't been lovers, but had there been affection? Did she yearn for him? Or for the mysterious Jean-Paul?

Huseyn swung around, pacing the room.

Ghizlan was *his*. For whatever reason, he couldn't now countenance any alternative. He had no intention of ending this marriage, which had given him everything he needed and more.

Which meant he had to overcome perhaps his greatest challenge—convincing his wife to act like a wife and not a prisoner of war.

Which meant wooing her.

Strangely, the notion appealed.

The prize—having proud, passionate Ghizlan reaching for him of her own volition, satisfying the gut-clenching hunger within—was irresistible.

He'd never had to exert himself to seduce a woman. He'd never had to flatter or even invite since women were only too eager to snare his attention. Relationships were purely sexual, easy and mutually satisfying.

Ghizlan was the only woman to spurn him. Perhaps that's why she intrigued him.

Or maybe because for the first time he was truly *interested*. From the beginning she'd attracted and infuriated him. Now he wanted to understand his contrary, accomplished, fascinating wife. She deserved his attention in her own right, not merely because of their marriage.

He stared at the closed door, remembering the gauntlet she'd flung down. A woman with her period wouldn't want physical seduction. What would she want? He had no idea. His was a man's world through and through. None of his lovers had ever discussed anything so intimate.

His mouth firmed. If she thought to scare him away by referring to such matters she was mistaken. He'd faced starvation, neglect and war. He'd faced down his dog of a father and demanded a chance at life. Everything he had he'd won through sheer determination.

He picked up the phone. His campaign began.

* * *

When Ghizlan emerged from the bathroom, warm from the shower and relaxed from the painkiller she'd taken, she found the bedroom filled with soft light from the lamps rather than the brilliant overhead chandelier. The bed was turned down and her maid had left a hot-water bottle. Had she guessed Ghizlan was suffering from cramps?

The last of Ghizlan's tension eased with the outward rush of her breath. Such peace after the storm. Thank goodness Huseyn had been scared by her mention of—

'You!' Her eyes rounded as the man himself strolled in from her sitting room, resplendent in loose, dark, low-slung trousers and nothing else.

Ghizlan's throat dried as if she'd swallowed part of the Great Sand Desert and her hands went to the sash of her robe, knotting it tight.

His eyebrows rose. 'You speak as if you expected some other man, when we both know you've never had anyone else in your bed.'

He sounded so smug she wanted to slap him. Except that would mean touching him and *that* was a mistake she wouldn't make again. Especially when he was shirtless, the brawny, golden expanse of his torso rugged and appallingly tempting with its dusting of dark hair, its deep bed of muscles and, she realised, seeing him properly for the first time, a collection of impressive scars. Was that an old *bullet* wound along his ribs?

'Why don't you get into bed?' He moved closer and she realised he was carrying a tray. From it came the heavenly aroma of cinnamon-spiced hot chocolate.

'It's too early.' She jutted her chin, falling back on the truth. 'And I don't want you here.'

He shrugged, those massive shoulders riding high in a fluid movement that glued her eyes to his magnificent form. For he really *was* magnificent. Powerfully built like some ancient god and potently male.

'You'll get used to me.' Blithely ignoring her fulminating stare, he put the tray on her bedside table. Not only hot chocolate but her other favourite, rare indulgence, delectable sugar syrup baklava, brimming with nuts and dripping sweetness.

Ghizlan's mouth watered.

Huseyn tugged back the bedcovers further and picked up the hot-water bottle. 'Why don't you indulge yourself? You're worn out. You can tell me off after you've rested. Right now you need warmth and something sweet.'

Ghizlan planted her hands on her hips in a show of defiance, ignoring the impulse to do exactly as he suggested. 'How would you know what I need?'

'I spoke to your maid.'

'You spoke…?'

'To your maid. She said you'd appreciate a hot-water bottle and a warm drink. The baklava was my idea.'

Ghizlan stared at the macho man before her. The warrior who drove all before him, who'd forced the Royal Council to name him Sheikh, who'd forged peace out of the beginnings of war and whose reputation as a hard man was second to none. *This* man had discussed her period with her maid? She'd been sure he'd run for the hills or one of his precious horses rather than think about such things.

'Here.' His touch on her arm was light but compelling. 'Let yourself relax for a bit, then you'll have the energy to fight with me again.'

Was that the shadow of a smile on his sculpted lips? No. He looked merely solicitous as he moved her towards the bed, tugging her off balance so she subsided unexpectedly onto the mattress. Before she had time to argue or get back on her feet, he'd swung her legs onto the bed and pressed the hot-water bottle into her hands, its warmth against her abdomen sheer luxury.

Despite herself Ghizlan subsided on a sigh of relief, clutching the hot-water bottle to her tummy.

'Is it always this bad?' He pulled the covers over her and she stared, undone by the novelty of Huseyn al Rasheed tucking her into bed as if he did it every day.

'No,' she found herself answering. 'Sometimes on the first day.' Ghizlan snapped her mouth shut. She hadn't intended to share even that. But the luxury of sinking into plump pillows, of warmth and softness, undermined caution.

She stared as Huseyn lifted the silver pot on the bedside table and poured the hot chocolate. His movements were economical, easy, as if this enormous bear of a man was quite at home. Of course he was! He ate and drank just like her. Yet the sight of that huge, scarred hand deftly managing the delicate pieces mesmerised her. Just as the scent of him, warm and richly male, and so foreign in her private sanctuary, tantalised.

'Don't you have a shirt to put on?' She sounded waspish. Good. Better than him thinking she accepted his presence.

He shrugged and Ghizlan fought not to stare at a delicious ripple of muscle. She'd never known a man's bare chest could be so distracting. But it wasn't just his chest. Those trousers sat so low she had a perfect view of taut abdominal muscles and the fine line of dark hair bisecting them.

'Be thankful I'm wearing pants. Usually I sleep nude.'

'You're not sleeping here!' She half sat and one large hand pressed her back down, gently but firmly.

'Not yet. I've ordered dinner to be brought here and then I've got several hours of work.'

'Then I suggest you do it elsewhere.' Ghizlan told herself she could do better than this. She should get out of bed, force him out...

But how? Huseyn wasn't going anywhere he didn't want to. She didn't have the physical strength to eject him and her ploy to scare him off by mentioning menstruation had backfired.

'Here. Try this.' He offered the hot chocolate, its rich scent curling through her.

Maybe he was right. Maybe she should recoup her strength before taking him on. Ghizlan slid higher in the bed, plumping the pillows behind her, and took the cup. His fingers brushed hers and runnels of liquid fire spread under her skin.

Obviously she was tired and imagining things.

'Thank you.' It hurt to say the words.

'My pleasure.' He strolled away, around the oversized bed to the other side where, she saw now, a vast wing chair had been placed. Beside it was a small table with a laptop and a pile of papers.

'What are you doing?'

'I told you I had work to do.' He sank into the chair, stretched his long, long legs and reached for the laptop. He caught her wide-eyed stare and his mouth flicked up at one corner. That hard, too-rugged face transformed as the hint of a dimple grooved one cheek. 'Yes, even we provincials can read and write.' Then he turned to the laptop.

Ghizlan shut her sagging mouth. She was about to snap that she hadn't for one minute thought him illiterate. It was more the unwanted *intimacy* of having Huseyn, bare-chested and barefoot, sprawled so casually beside her bed.

Shouldn't he be inspecting his troops or managing some crisis or doing whatever it was that kept his body in such amazing shape?

'That hot chocolate will get cold if you don't drink it.' He didn't even look up. Was she so easy to second-guess? The thought infuriated. Rather than waste effort sparring, she sank back, sipping the delicious drink, and told herself she'd deal with him later.

But later there was no dealing with him. After indulging in an unheard-of rest, Ghizlan was refreshed enough to eat dinner and tackle some of her own paperwork. But as the evening wore on tiredness claimed her and she found herself dozing, the business plan for the perfume factory spread on her lap.

She woke as Huseyn moved the papers away. Amazing to think she'd relaxed enough to forget he was in the room. Not forget precisely, but there'd been something unaccountably reassuring about hearing the quiet shuffle of papers and the soft rhythm of his fingers on his keyboard.

Blearily she looked up into misty blue eyes fringed with thick dark lashes. How had she never noticed how beautiful they were?

Because she'd been too busy watching them narrow in annoyance or disapproval.

'Sleep now, Ghizlan.'

She moved to lift the sheet and sit up but his hand, hot on her shoulder, stopped her. 'Don't fret. I promise to let you sleep undisturbed.'

Dazed, looking up into that open stare, Ghizlan found herself believing him. Slowly she sank back, part of her brain warning that giving in was a mistake. But it was smothered by tiredness. She'd worked non-stop the last few weeks, stressed over the peace talks, wondering about the outcome, and determined to support her people by being seen, calm and supportive, as often as possible. Her schedule had been a nightmare.

Nevertheless, she lay rigid, listening as he put her papers on the table and switched off her lamp. Her breath caught as he moved but it was only to return to the wing chair and his work.

For long minutes Ghizlan watched him, wondering how the line of his broken nose, the firm slash of his mouth and that solid, uncompromising jaw could look so attractive. As for his shoulders and chest, the torso tapering to narrow hips…she shut her eyes rather than let her gaze wander there.

When she opened them again it was broad daylight. She'd slept far later than usual and the sun was high. She lay, disorientated, until memories of last night flooded back and she turned her head to the other side of the vast bed. It was empty, and, when she stretched out a hand, cold. Yet there was a dent in the pillow where Huseyn's head had rested and his male scent reached her as she moved.

He'd invaded her space, her privacy, even her bed, and she'd let him.

Had he really meant what he'd said? That he'd wait till she invited him to make love to her?

Her lips compressed as she swung her legs out of bed. She might have a weakness for Huseyn's kisses but even she wasn't so stupid as to think he'd ever made love to her. It had been sex. Raw and unvarnished. And if he thought one evening's solicitousness could make her change her mind he was in for a nasty shock.

When she returned to her room—their room—that evening, it was a relief to find it empty. Huseyn had flown to a city on the other side of the country. With her luck he'd return after she was asleep. The thought of seeing that big, golden body half naked and sprawled in her space sent a shiver through her.

Over a cup of mint tea she chatted on the phone to Arden, the Englishwoman who'd married Sheikh Idris of Zahrat, abruptly ending Ghizlan's almost-betrothal. Both women had weathered the storm of scandal that followed and built a rapport, then a friendship. Of course Ghizlan had Mina too, but her sister was years younger and busy with her studies and the delights of France. Besides, Ghizlan and Arden shared similar lives, being sheikhas of neighbouring countries.

The sound of the sitting room door opening made her swing round and there was Huseyn, his long legs eating up the space between them. Ghizlan's heart jolted against her breastbone.

'I'll have to go now.'

'He's back, is he?' Arden sounded intrigued. 'One day you'll have to bring him to Zahrat so I can meet him. I've heard amazing stories about him—the iron warrior and all that, but I know there must be more to him since you married him.'

Ghizlan bit down a sour laugh. She hadn't told Arden the true nature of her marriage and didn't intend to. Not over the phone at any rate. 'That sounds good,' she murmured, aware of Huseyn behind her. 'I'll call later.'

'Your sister?' She hunched her shoulders as that deep, velvety voice ran across her sensitised nerves.

'Just a friend.' She turned and stopped, aghast, to see him reefing off his clothes.

'What?' He paused, registering her stare. Was that amusement in his eyes?

'I'd prefer not to watch you undress.'

'Then avert your eyes, my lady.' With that he stripped off his trousers and underwear to stand breathtakingly naked.

Ghizlan blinked, telling herself not to look as he crossed to the bathroom. Yet heat blazed in her cheeks as he shut the door. It wasn't just the lithe grace of his movements— a man utterly at ease with his body. It was also the size of him…there. How had they ever fitted together? No wonder it had hurt. Statues she'd seen of naked men had always looked rather limp in that area. Whereas Huseyn looked almost primed for…

She swung away, grabbing her laptop and heading for the sitting room. Work would keep her mind off…him.

Later, at his insistence, they ate dinner in their private dining room. Why he wanted to be with her, Ghizlan couldn't understand. He sure wasn't trying to seduce her. His responses to her few efforts at conversation were short and his mouth tight.

'I'm sorry.' The surprising words jerked her head up. 'I've been like a bear with a sore head.'

Ghizlan raised her eyebrows but refused to ask for details.

'Dealing with some of your officials is an exercise in frustration.'

'*My* officials?'

His mouth lifted at one corner and Ghizlan wished she didn't find the sight so ridiculously attractive. Those occasional hints of humour were too disarming.

'Okay. Representatives of *our* national parliament. I've spent all day trying to get two of them to work together but it's futile.'

'Why bother? Why not order them to obey?' It's what she'd have expected a few weeks ago, before she'd seen the way he'd negotiated a truce with Halarq and convinced even the most bellicose of those in government that discussion rather than confrontation was the way to go.

'I could, but I'd prefer them to negotiate amongst themselves. In the longer run it will save work and time if they're not sending every decision up the line to me.'

He was delegating, reinforcing the role of officials to take responsibility for their decisions. Not demanding every decision be his.

'What is it? You're looking at me strangely.'

Ghizlan shook her head. It wouldn't improve his mood if she told him she was surprised he trusted anyone but himself to make decisions. She was rapidly revising her assumption that his bid for power was all about ego.

'Who's proving so difficult?'

'The Ministers for Education and for Public Works.'

'Ah.' That explained it.

Huseyn sat forward. 'Ah, what?'

'They can't stand each other.'

'Go on.'

'My father used to keep them apart as much as possible but they're both excellent at their jobs, so he didn't want to move them.' She paused, seeing Huseyn waiting for more. 'There was a family rift. One of them had been on the verge of a betrothal when he fell in love with the woman's sister. The marriage contract was changed so he could marry the younger sister. Relations between the women have been strained since and when the older sister married the feud continued.'

'The two bridegrooms are our two ministers?' He shook his head. 'They're well into their fifties. Surely this happened decades ago?'

'Yes, but neither man liked the other anyway. Father said they have very different personalities. One is a methodical planner and the other is instinctive, taking risks others wouldn't.'

She looked up to find those pale eyes fixed on her. 'Your father used to discuss a lot with you.'

Ghizlan shrugged. 'Mainly with Azim, his chief adviser, but, yes, I picked up a lot.'

'He trusted you.' His statement made Ghizlan pause. She'd been frustrated by her father's determination to use her as a political tool and hurt by his inability to *love* her. Yet he'd spoken to her about his work as if she were clever enough to understand and contribute. She'd never thought about it before, but in his own way he'd at least respected her, even if he'd been too emotionally barren to have a normal relationship with her.

'Ghizlan?'

She blinked and looked up into that piercing stare. 'Sorry, my mind was wandering.' And her emotions. Maybe it was hormonal but abruptly she felt her father's loss. He'd been far from a perfect parent but neither had he been a monster. Now he was gone, the only parent she remembered.

'Please excuse me.' She pushed back her chair. 'I'm tired.' It was too early to sleep but she needed privacy.

Maybe Huseyn realised for he didn't follow her into the bedroom. For two hours Ghizlan worked her way through the documents requiring her attention, hoping work would blanket the grief that had overtaken her. It helped, yet still she felt drawn and sad. Finally, packing up her papers, she reached for a paperback. With luck she could lose herself in a good story.

'You're reading a *book*?' Huseyn's inflection made it sound unexpected. Ghizlan looked up, carefully keeping her eyes trained on his face as he undressed. That little skitter of excitement deep inside was surely a bad sign. As was the quickened patter of her pulse.

'I've finished my work and this helps me relax.'

He strode closer. Did he *have* to be bare-chested? Was he trying to remind her how she'd enjoyed touching him? Ghizlan dragged her gaze back to the book.

'You like reading about sex?'

Her head shot up and their gazes meshed. Heat drilled to her core, swirling there in an ache that had nothing to do with her period. She shifted in the bed, stopping abruptly as his eyes narrowed. Could he read her body so easily? Did he know that just the word *sex* on his lips had her remembering the awesome power of their coupling? The urgency for fulfilment that had made a mockery of her denials? Even the disappointing outcome couldn't banish the memory of how wonderful it had been in the beginning.

Ghizlan turned the book to look at its cover. A woman in ringlets and a long gown arched into the embrace of a man in tight breeches and boots. The man was missing his shirt and Ghizlan couldn't help comparing his glossy, hairless chest with that of the man before her. Huseyn looked powerful, huskily male and so desirable her fingers twitched with the need to touch him.

'Not sex. Love.' Her voice sounded strangled and she cleared her throat. 'Well, there's sex in there too but ultimately it's about love.'

'Love?' Huseyn frowned as if she'd spoken a foreign language. 'Is that what you want from life?'

'No.' She'd always known she wouldn't have that luxury. Except for a too-short period when she'd dreamed of escaping with Mina and living a life of her own devising. 'I know love isn't for me.'

'But you believe in it?'

Why was he interested? He stood so close her nostrils quivered at the lush, male scent of him. The calm she'd found reading the historical romance evaporated. How could she relax with him looming over her, half naked?

'I believe it exists. But really, I'm just reading to relax so I sleep.' He opened his mouth and she rushed on, needing to change the subject. 'What do you read?'

'Petitions, proposals, plans.' He shrugged and, to her relief, walked towards the bathroom.

'I mean for pleasure.' Why she was curious she didn't understand. Did she really want to know her husband?

'I've never read for pleasure.'

'Never...?' Ghizlan stared. 'But that's...'

'Reading was a skill I learned because I needed it.' His expression was unreadable. 'It's useful. That's all.'

Before she could question him further he entered the bathroom and shut the door, leaving her pondering a life without the joy of reading. Somehow it fitted her original impression of Huseyn—a warrior, tough and uncompromising, with no time for the finer things in life. But she knew now he was more complex than that. He could even be kind.

Ghizlan had thought she'd sleep well, but her mind circled again and again over intriguing new insights about her father and her husband. Even when Huseyn had finished his own work and turned out the light she lay, trying to turn off the thoughts humming through her brain. She rolled over again.

'What's wrong?' Huseyn's voice was a soft rumble behind her. She'd thought him asleep.

'Nothing. I'm just not sleepy.'

'That's what comes from reading about sex before bed.'

'I didn't…' Ghizlan subsided in a huff. There was no point discussing it. Huseyn would believe what he wanted. 'I've got some things on my mind.' Like her unwilling fascination for her husband and the fact he was far less brutal and far more intriguing than was good for her.

'There's a cure for that.' His voice held a note that ran like fire through her veins.

She'd bet there was. 'I don't want sex.'

'I wasn't offering it.' His tone bordered on smug and her palm itched to slap him. Except that would mean rolling over and touching him and—

Her breath escaped in a squeak of shock as she felt heat behind her and a powerful arm wrapped around her middle, drawing her across the bed.

'What do you think you're—?' Her words stopped as she collided with his body. It curved around her, knees to the backs of her knees, groin to her bottom, solid chest to her back. An arm slid under her head and Ghizlan found herself cushioned by hot, living muscle. Worse was the unmistakably rigid shaft that lay against her buttocks. Huseyn was aroused. So aroused her stomach dipped and quivered in what she told herself was horror. It could not, absolutely could *not* be excitement.

'Making you comfortable so you can sleep.'

'You really think I'll be able to sleep like this?'

'Others have. It's something to do with the comfort of lying against another body.'

Ghizlan swallowed. How many women had taken comfort from Huseyn's body? She screwed up her eyes. She didn't want to know. 'Let me go.' She shoved at his arm but it didn't budge. 'I'd rather sleep alone.'

'But you weren't sleeping, were you? You were keeping me awake. I have a lot to do tomorrow. I need my rest.'

Feeling guilty, Ghizlan lay rigid till eventually his breathing slowed and she felt the rhythm of his breaths in the subtle movement of his body embracing her. It was like being in a hammock, swaying gently, she thought muzzily before finally slipping into oblivion, her hand around the sinewy forearm that held her securely.

Into the night Huseyn lay watching the moon's progress. Lying with Ghizlan was exquisite torture. When she snuffled and burrowed against him his groin caught fire and only his promise not to take her held him still. He'd already broken his earlier promise—not to hurt her. He'd keep his word now. But the combination of tantalising body and sharp mind made his bride daily more rather than less alluring. That had never happened with any other woman.

Huseyn frowned, telling himself that once this became a real marriage, this fascination would lessen and he'd be able to concentrate again.

CHAPTER ELEVEN

TEN DAYS LATER Ghizlan looked across the dining table at the man she'd married and to her shock realised she was *easy* in his company.

It had been a slow process, but inexorable. If she didn't go to sleep with his arm around her she'd wake up in his embrace with no memory of having shifted in the night. Those embraces were a two-edged sword. To her surprise she loved snuggling into his heat, feeling safe as if nothing bad in the world could touch her. Which was bizarre since she was his captive. At the same time her restlessness increased. The stirring deep within spoke of sexual hunger.

But this...acceptance was more than physical. He'd begun asking her opinion about issues that arose during his day and asking about hers. She was growing comfortable as they discussed the one thing that really linked them: their work for Jeirut.

Huseyn looked up. 'What's wrong?'

'Nothing.' She paused, aware of the dragging sensation in her stomach when his misty blue eyes met hers. Despite sharing a bed, he'd kept his word, never demanding sex. Which surely proved he didn't really want her.

Except every night she felt him press against her, making her wonder what it would be like if she invited him—

'Ghizlan?'

She shook her head. 'You never did tell me what happened between you and the Emir of Halarq's nephew when you met on the border. How did you persuade him to champion a peace deal?'

Huseyn watched her so long she thought he might not

answer. Did he guess she was diverting the subject? Finally he shrugged and helped himself to a dish of chicken with pomegranate.

'He's ambitious and eager for prestige, like his uncle. But he's intelligent too. He soon realised the consequences for his country if they attacked. They'd hoped to grab territory while Jeirut was without a leader, but I made it clear I was in control and wouldn't sit idle.' He shrugged. 'Unlike his uncle, his head isn't filled with dreams. The old man deludes himself with visions of honour and great warriors, but real war isn't like that.'

'You speak from experience.' Ghizlan remembered the silvered scars on his torso, her gaze dropping to the marks on his hand as he lifted a forkful of food to his mouth.

His world was so different. Yet he was surprisingly easy to talk with. As if he wasn't her enemy at all.

'I grew up on the border. I experienced raids by the Emir's *gallant* warriors.' Sarcasm laced his tone and an underlying roughness hinted at strong emotions. 'They specialised in attacking at night, terrorising peaceful villagers, looting and raping and…'

'And?' Ghizlan heard the thread of suppressed emotion in his voice. She put down her cutlery and leaned forward.

'One night when I was six they came to our village. My mother lifted me out the window and told me to run to our hiding place in the foothills. It was too late for adults to escape, but skinny little kids could slip through the shadows. Next door Selim's mother did the same, asking me to look after him because he was a child.'

And a six-year-old wasn't a child? Ghizlan's throat tightened. 'Selim? Not—?'

Huseyn nodded. 'Our Captain of the Guard, yes. We grew up together.'

The bond between the two was strong. Ghizlan knew Huseyn trusted the other man implicitly and that Selim was unquestionably loyal. 'What happened?'

Huseyn stabbed a chunk of meat with his fork then put it down. 'We returned at daybreak. We already knew this raid was worse. We'd seen the smoke. The village had been destroyed and it was empty. They took the survivors across the border as forced labour.' His voice was unnaturally blank when he continued. 'We found six bodies, including Selim's parents and my mother. It took us all day to bury them.'

Ghizlan's heart contracted. How could she not have known this sort of thing had happened on their border? Why had her father not told her? Because of the bad blood between him and Huseyn's father that had kept relations with the province of Jumeah so strained? Because he'd sought to protect her?

'I'm so very sorry.' The words were totally inadequate.

'It was a long time ago.' He met her stare, his own clouded. She wanted to reach out and comfort him. As if this self-contained man would welcome that!

'What happened then?'

'You want the story of my life?' His brows crunched together.

'Why not? Unless you prefer that I rely on the stories I hear.'

He waved a dismissive hand. 'People exaggerate.' He paused then went on in a matter-of-fact tone. 'It took us a few days but we made it to the capital. Then, on the day my father held his public audience, I confronted him and asked him to take us in.'

'And he did.' How could he not?

Huseyn laughed, the sound mirthless. 'No, he told me to get lost. My father had sired many bastards and didn't care. He didn't recall seducing my mother when she'd worked as a servant in his home. He'd enjoyed many women and debauching an innocent girl meant nothing to him.'

Their eyes met and Ghizlan's throat tightened. Was that how he thought of their wedding night? Was that why he'd taken such trouble to show another, gentler side of himself, because he felt guilty over taking her virginity?

'His guards were moving us away when I shouted that he was a man without honour. That I'd be better crossing the border and throwing myself on the mercy of his enemy, the Emir of Halarq.' Huseyn's mouth lifted in a bitter smile. 'That shocked the room to silence. I thought he'd order the guards to chop off my head.'

'But it worked.'

Huseyn sat back, rolling his shoulders as if releasing an old stiffness. 'After a fashion. He hated me but didn't turn us away. He set us to work in the stables. We'd bed down with the horses and spend every waking hour working. Eventually his guards accepted us. They liked us enough to teach us some fighting skills when we begged. We practised and practised until finally one of them decided we'd be more use as soldiers than stable hands.'

'And you worked your way through the ranks.'

He nodded. 'I was determined to be the best. I devoted every waking hour to perfecting my skills, learning what I could, including reading and writing late at night. I became a lieutenant, then a commander and finally my father realised I wasn't just one of his best soldiers, but the only man who could take his place when he died and keep the province safe. Believe me, that was a grudging decision.'

'You really did earn everything you got.' Ghizlan's thoughts whirled, trying to imagine what it must have taken to mould himself into the man he was now.

'Except, you would say, the Sheikhdom of Jeirut.' His stare was steady, acknowledging rather than challenging.

Ghizlan waited for the familiar throb of fury that he'd taken her father's place. But it didn't come, not with the force she expected. She chose her words carefully. 'I never disputed your right to be Sheikh.'

He was proving himself a strong, fair ruler, even if he had a lot to learn about the complex layers of responsibility involved in running a nation. None of the other contenders for the position could have done better, she realised.

'Just my right to take you as my bride.' Was it imagination or did that gaze sizzle with silvery heat?

Ghizlan looked down, pushing the half-eaten meal around her plate, her feelings in turmoil. It had been so easy to despise him as a bullying oaf. Now she was faced with a more complicated man. One potentially more dangerous to her peace of mind.

'What you did was unconscionable.'

'Even for the good of the country?'

She felt the tug of reason, of duty and royal responsibility. Hadn't she been trained from birth to act, not for herself, but for the good of the nation?

Ghizlan shot him a look. 'You can't expect *me* to applaud a forced marriage. Anyway, it's a little too late to ask the victim for absolution.'

'Victim?' He swirled his water goblet thoughtfully. 'Is that what you are? I thought you were stronger than that.' Pale eyes coupled with hers. 'I thought you revelled in your role as Sheikha. I couldn't imagine anyone else doing it with such panache or dedication.'

Power arced between them, pinioning her in her seat. It wasn't just the dazzle of those remarkable eyes, it was something else, some force that welded her to the spot.

His approval? Is that what makes you so weak? Because he compliments you on doing your duty?

'It never occurred to you that I wanted to do something else with my life? That I yearned for the day I could make my *own* life? Set my *own* goals?'

It was nonsense, of course. She'd been destined for a dynastic marriage from birth. Only in those few brief days after her father's death had she known the heady excitement of perhaps choosing for herself. Yet she resented the way Huseyn had robbed her of that.

He leaned close, every line of his big frame attentive. 'What would you have chosen to do, Ghizlan?'

The sorry truth was she had no idea. That made her angrier than ever. At herself. Had she been so subsumed by her royal role she couldn't even *dream* for herself?

Suddenly the conversation was too much. She pushed her chair back. 'I have work to do. If you'll excuse me.'

Huseyn delayed joining her in the bedroom, instead visiting the stables. There was something calming about horses. They either accepted you or they didn't. They were honest and loyal, usually more than people.

He took up a curry comb and began to groom his favourite grey stallion, the rhythm of the action soothing.

Had Ghizlan really dreamt of another life? With Idris of Zahrat or the mysterious Jean-Paul? Bitterness filled his gullet at the thought of her with someone else.

He told himself it couldn't matter now. The die was cast. She was his and he wasn't letting her go.

Yet guilt bit. What right had he to deny her dreams? His own dream had been simple. Survival. That's why he'd stood up to his father as a six-year-old in front of a court of mocking adults. Why he'd worked tirelessly in the stables then as a soldier. To survive, and keep his friend Selim alive too. That meant being strong, the strongest of all. If he was the strongest no one could touch him unless they killed him in battle and that was a price he'd always been prepared to pay.

But Ghizlan touched him in ways he'd never imagined, made him feel things he didn't have names for. She even made him wonder if his strength was enough.

More and more he learned from her. He could lead men into battle and even, it seemed, toward peace. But daily he discovered new complexities in his royal role. From advisers but as often from Ghizlan, who had an unerring instinct for politics and good governance.

If she'd been male, Jeirut would have been lucky to have her inherit the throne.

The differences between them struck him again like the kick of an untamed horse. He was rough, tough and baseborn. Ghizlan was refined and well bred. Who could blame her if she pined for Idris as a husband? She'd spoken of having her own goals. Had that been one?

Huseyn's jaw tightened. Marrying him must have been the stuff of nightmares. He tried to imagine what she'd felt—not the spoiled, selfish socialite he'd thought her, but the honourable, hard-working, cultured woman who put duty first.

His skin crawled at what his imagination conjured and he swore, long and low, till the stallion turned and nuzzled him, its dark eye sympathetic.

Huseyn huffed a mirthless laugh.

He mightn't deserve Ghizlan but she was his now. Could he earn her respect? Make her happy? She deserved that.

When he returned to their room she was absorbed in paperwork, not, as usual, in bed, but at the small desk by the window he'd never seen her use. Making a point about keeping her distance? Disappointment stirred. Surely he'd win her over eventually? At least they'd moved from confrontation to a truce.

When he emerged from the shower and found her lying in bed, absorbed in another of those romance books, he smiled. Huseyn liked sharing a bed with Ghizlan, even if it was torment, lying with her and not sating the constant, urgent desire for her.

'What's this?' Beside his chair, on top of the pile of paperwork waiting for him, were some books. He picked up the first, its cover black with gold lettering.

'I thought you might like to read something different.' He turned to see Ghizlan watching him, her expression guarded. 'There's an action bestseller and a non-fiction.'

Huseyn stared, first at her, then at the thick paperback in his hand. He shut his eyes for a second as his skin tingled all over and an unfamiliar sensation churned his belly. He opened them again, staring at but not taking in the words on the cover.

'Huseyn? Are you okay?'

He nodded, not looking up. Not wanting her to see what he now recognised as shock. 'Of course.' He paused, swallowing heavily. 'Thank you. That's…thoughtful of you.' He couldn't quite comprehend it. Did this mean she didn't regard him as the enemy, despite their earlier conversation?

'You're welcome.'

He waited a couple of seconds before looking in her direction. To his relief she'd turned back to her book and he sank into his chair, aware that his knees were loose as if he'd taken a heavy blow. Slowly he breathed out.

His reaction was ridiculous. They were only books.

But they were the first gift he'd ever received.

Growing up on the edge of starvation, he'd never expected presents. In recent years, though he didn't want for material things, everything he had he'd earned. Even the provincial sheikhdom his father had reluctantly bequeathed to him. He'd earned it with his blood and toil and every ounce of his being.

He stroked the cover of the paperback gently.

'It wouldn't hurt you to take a night off and open a book instead.'

He shafted a look across the room but Ghizlan was already turning her attention back to her own reading.

Had she seen his hesitation? His awe?

He was tempted to put the books aside and open them when he was alone but that smacked of cowardice. Slowly he opened the bestseller.

Fifteen minutes later she spoke again. 'If you're not enjoying it, try the other one.'

Huseyn jerked his head up. How had she known?

At his stare she smiled. 'You've been tsking and tutting almost from the first page.'

'I have?' He hadn't been aware of it. 'It's just a little...' he searched for an acceptable word '...far-fetched. If he'd stabbed the man in the spot he describes then he would have died within seconds and the killer would have been sprayed with blood. The victim couldn't have lingered so long, telling his secrets to the person who found him.'

'I really don't want to know how you know that.' Ghizlan shook her head. 'Why not try the other one?'

Huseyn hesitated. He didn't want her to think he didn't value her gift.

'Please? I had no idea what you'd enjoy. Maybe you'll like the other more.'

He did, he discovered. It was a history of Jeirut and the first chapter was about the prehistoric remains he hadn't known were dotted around the region. Fascinated, he lost track of time until he heard Ghizlan's light click off.

Huseyn sat back, thoughts racing. This evening had been remarkable. For the unfamiliar feelings Ghizlan evoked. Then for the way she had knocked him off balance with her precious gift and finally with the discovery he felt relaxed, intrigued and at peace after reading.

He slanted a look at the bed and found her watching him through slitted eyes. He swallowed hard. Always it was difficult resisting the physical temptation of her, but tonight it would be almost impossible. Not only was she beautiful and clever, she had grace and unexpected kindness even in the face of all he'd done.

'Thank you, Ghizlan.' His voice was gravel.

'My pleasure.' Then she rolled over, turning her back.

An hour later Huseyn was still awake. Not surprising since he habitually spent so many hours fighting his animal urges with Ghizlan in his arms. But tonight it was she who was restless even with his outstretched arm as a pillow, which she usually enjoyed. She didn't twitch or shift away, but she lay stiff as a board, her tension palpable.

'Relax,' he murmured, inhaling her sweet scent.

'I'm sorry. I'm keeping you awake. I just can't settle.' She made to roll away but he hooked his arm around her waist, holding her on her back.

'Stay.' Her ribcage rose above his arm as she drew a shuddery breath and he wondered if perhaps Ghizlan too was victim to the strange tug of feelings tonight. Or was she fretting over some distant lover?

Huseyn's jaw tensed. 'I can help you relax.' He lifted his arm, letting his hand graze the soft cotton covering her ribs.

She shook her head, that silky hair splaying over his arm. 'I don't want sex. I think it's better if I—'

'This wouldn't be sex.' He let his hand drift to her breast, plump and perfect, and heard her hiss of indrawn breath. Delicately he circled before cupping her breast, letting it fill his palm. Fire shot straight to his already over-heated groin and he gritted his teeth.

He'd waited so long. Wanted her so long.

Okay, it would be sex, but not full sex, so it wasn't a lie. And he was doing this for her, he told himself.

When he gently pinched her nipple she gave a soft, choked cry and almost lifted off the bed. He slid his leg over hers, anchoring her to the bed, though interestingly she showed no sign of fighting him.

'Huseyn!' Her voice was high and throaty, and it did dreadful things to his self-control. 'This is a bad idea. I don't—'

'Let me do this for you,' he said against the cotton covering her breast, then before she could answer, he took her breast in his mouth, suckling hard.

Her moan of delight was everything he could have wished. He wanted to strip away the simple nightgown she wore so he could feast on her skin but he didn't want to scare her. Instead he concentrated on worshiping at one full, delectable breast, then the other, until she was writhing and her breath came in little pants punctuated by throaty moans that made him wonder if he might explode just at the sound of her. His erection, his whole lower body was like forged steel, fiery hot and impossibly hard.

'Huseyn!'

He shifted, looking up to meet her eyes, and desire detonated. Her hips were lifting in time with his caress and he felt her rising excitement. He arrowed his hand down, dragging up her nightdress until his fingers touched the satiny skin of her inner thighs. Instead of stiffening, they fell apart for him, allowing him access to her damp core.

Still their eyes held as he found her centre, stroked her, first softly, then hard and she arched back into the bed, her hips rising, her breathing almost a sob.

'Huseyn, I…'

'It's all right, my lovely. It's all right. Just let go.' And to his delight she did, just as he slid his finger into that slick inner passage. She contracted hard and fast again and again, and all the time he watched her face, enthralled by the sight of her overcome by the pleasure he gave her.

A great shudder shook him as he slowly withdrew, then pulled his arm from beneath her head. She tested his honour as it had never been tested. Maybe he should go to the stables again, or check the night watch, or—

'Where are you going?' Her voice was velvet, trawling across nerve endings so tense he feared for his control.

'You'll sleep now, Ghizlan.' He pushed back the covers and levered himself up. Except one soft hand closed around his biceps.

He swung round. She was sitting up, her hair a dark cloud around her shoulders, her eyes, even in this dim light, sparkling like stars.

'You need to let me go.' He could break her hold if he

wanted to. But he didn't want to. And he feared what might happen if he touched her again. He'd given his word that he'd wait for her to ask.

'No. I won't.'

CHAPTER TWELVE

'I DON'T WANT you to go.' The words came out in a rush of relief, like air from a punctured balloon. Ghizlan's lungs swelled and filled as the tightness she'd been nursing for weeks eased.

She'd fought this, him, so long...no, fought *herself*. She'd tried to tell herself she didn't want him. That it was a betrayal to want him. But nothing worked. Self-denial had its limits and she'd reached hers.

'I want you,' she whispered, her grip tightening on that biceps that bulged beneath her touch. The admission should have felt like defeat but it tasted like victory. Like a woman acknowledging her desires unashamedly. She desired Huseyn as she had no other man.

She hadn't intended this. Especially tonight when she'd been so confused by the question of what she really wanted from life. But when he'd walked into their suite, rumpled and dusty and smelling of horse, she'd been hard put not to follow him into the bathroom and ask him to kiss her. And when he'd seen the gift she'd put out... The wonder in his eyes, the unguarded emotion that chased across his face, had touched something deep within.

Callused fingers stroked her cheek and she could have sworn sparks ignited from his touch. She cupped her hand to his, pressing it against her face. His hand was big and hard, like Huseyn. But it could be incredibly gentle too. She understood that now.

His gaze searched hers, questioning. She tried to smile but her facial muscles were too tight. Instead she lay down, clasping his hand to her face. 'I want you, Huseyn.'

His features grew taut and his breathing roughened. She

planted her other hand square on that massive chest, shaping the broad band of muscle, skimming the light covering of hair that so fascinated her. Strange how his size no longer threatened her.

To her delight he snatched a sharp breath and beneath her palm his heartbeat pounded.

'You're sure?' His voice was unrecognisable and Ghizlan revelled in the discovery of her power. It made her feel vibrant and beautiful. Not like a woman married for her pedigree but like one he couldn't resist.

Before she had time to think she grabbed the hem of her nightgown and, with a wiggle of hips to free it, reefed it over her head.

Cool air caressed her bare skin as he held still, watching. He sat like that so long her hands crept up to cover her breasts. Instantly his fingers closed on her wrists, gently pulling her arms wide, leaving her completely bare to his gaze. Her breasts rose with each quickened breath and between her legs heat flared anew. She felt self-conscious and at the same time triumphant.

With a guttural groan he lowered himself, his chest against hers so exquisitely arousing that she couldn't keep still. Until his mouth closed on hers and all else faded. His lips were almost reverential as they stroked hers. Their breaths mingled and it was the sweetest, most profoundly moving experience.

His tongue stroked into her mouth and she sighed her delight. Need shuddered through her and she hugged him tight, curving her body into his. The fine cotton of his pants might as well not have been there as she rubbed against that powerful erection, driven by a need she could no longer resist.

With a groan he broke their kiss and slid down her body to capture her breast in his mouth. It was delicious, addictive but not what she wanted.

'Please, Huseyn. I want you.'

In answer he moved again, but lower, hooking her knees up so they splayed either side of his head. Ghizlan blinked, trying to tell herself she wasn't shocked at the sight of his dark head there, or the heat of his breath in that most intimate of places.

Then his head dipped and thought stopped. He'd given her an orgasm before but nothing had prepared her for the carnal power of this caress. She shivered with each touch, each decadent lick, and couldn't take her eyes off him. Abruptly that quake of sensation erupted, starting as tiny ripples and building and building until it consumed her and she flung her head back, crying out his name, clutching at his head with fingers knotted in ecstasy.

Later Ghizlan felt limp, wrecked and elated, her body racked by aftershocks as he moved up the bed, his eyes holding hers. Despite the thrills still coursing through her, the hectic pulse at her core, she'd never wanted anything as much as she wanted this man.

He leaned over her, propped on strong arms so as not to crush her, his breath feathering her. She wanted him closer.

'Better?' She felt the word against her collarbone as he kissed her there. It was the only place they touched, apart from her feet at his ankles, and it wasn't enough.

'It was wonderful,' she gasped. 'But it wasn't what I wanted.' She lifted her hands, curling them around his shoulders and tugging. 'It's you I want. All of you.'

Sated as she was, accepting she couldn't possibly climax again, she wanted that unfamiliar, mind-boggling connection she'd experienced only once.

'Ah, Ghizlan.' There was need in that gravelly whisper and it urged her to take what she wanted. Her hands went to the drawstring of his loose trousers, tugging it undone, sliding the fabric down his hips so he lay hot and rigid against her.

How could that feel like heaven when he'd taken her there twice already? He moved, positioning himself at her core yet still holding back, his face furrowed in concentration, or was that restraint? Did he fear hurting her again?

Boldly she slid her hands round his hips and over his taut, rounded buttocks. They flexed at her touch and her fingers tightened as tentatively she lifted her pelvis.

Ghizlan sighed as he slid forward, that incredible heat filling her slowly, so slowly it was delicious torment. She flexed her fingers and angled her hips higher and saw Huseyn squeeze his eyes shut as he sank deeper.

'Are you all right?'

His mouth twisted up at one corner. 'I should be asking you that.'

Ghizlan stilled, cataloguing the amazing sensation of them together. 'Wonderful, except I want more.'

The words were barely out when he drove in, smoothly but inexorably right to the centre of her and she forgot how to speak.

Gleaming eyes met hers. 'Okay?'

She nodded, breath caught as he moved away, infinitely slowly, till she thought he'd withdraw completely and dug her fingers hard into his flesh. She wrapped one leg up over his, trying to keep him where he was.

He smiled then, but not *at* her. She sensed that for the first time they were totally attuned. That was borne out when he sank into her again and her moan of delight mingled with his deep, guttural groan.

'What should I do?' she whispered when she found her voice.

'Nothing!' She caught the gleam of his teeth as he grimaced. 'Or I won't be able to wait for you to come.'

Huseyn's mouth closed on hers, his tongue delving deep as he withdrew then thrust again, faster this time, a little harder, creating a fizz of excitement she'd thought impossible.

His rhythm was regular yet with a gradually increasing tempo that pushed her closer and closer to that unseen edge. His bulk surrounding her, his salty male scent, his mouth on hers, the bunch and release of muscles beneath her hands, were a potent combination that accelerated pleasure. Ghizlan held tight, kissing him back, giving herself to the rhythm that had taken over her body until on one solid thrust he drove her to a pinnacle unlike any she'd experienced. Bliss was there, waves of tight, bright pleasure, and Huseyn was there too, strong, hard and vital, right at the heart of her.

Ghizlan shattered with a cry and it was as if Huseyn had waited for a signal. The long, rhythmic thrusts became a quick, hungry bucking that drove him hard into her, amazingly prolonging her climax.

Then with a hoarse shout Huseyn arched his neck back, his face fierce yet vulnerable as he lost control and spilled himself inside her.

It must be the clouds of ecstasy, the rush of endorphins filling her, but at that moment Ghizlan felt a profound oneness with him. She lifted her arms, pulling him down until his head sank into the curve of her shoulder, his panting breath against her skin. She never wanted this to end.

Huseyn woke to the sun high in the sky and a sense of wellbeing so intense he realised he was smiling. He'd never known anything like it.

Because of the woman snuggled in his hold, her hair a silken blanket across his chest. Beautiful, passionate, generous Ghizlan. Despite her exhaustion she'd been eager for him when he'd caressed her awake twice more in the night. She'd given herself unstintingly and each time it had been difficult to ensure her satisfaction before his because his hunger for her grew with each embrace instead of lessening. Only the fact she was still new to sex had held him back from more. He'd held her in his arms for hours, amazed at how much he enjoyed cuddling her, until he'd finally succumbed to sleep at dawn.

It was long past time he was up and about his duties but for the first time in his life Huseyn lay abed. Duty could wait. The sheikhdom wouldn't crumble if he was late today.

He lay there, rough hands on tender flesh, and knew he was the luckiest man alive. It wasn't just the sex. It was Ghizlan. His confounding, obstinate, talented, clever, smart-mouthed, kind wife. Being with her made him feel... better. Not that he'd ever been aware of a lack in his life. All he knew was that now he had her nothing would make him relinquish her. He might have won her through force and blackmail but he'd bind her to him with whatever ties he could.

There wasn't a flicker of doubt, no voice warning about being in thrall to a woman. Because even a man who'd lived his whole life in a rough, brutal man's world, who'd never wanted or expected to want a woman for anything more than sexual release, knew when he held treasure.

He'd set out to tame her, dominate her. But what he really wanted was to win her. To earn her trust and her—

A scratching sound on the sitting room door caught his attention. 'My lady?' It was Ghizlan's maid.

Carefully extricating himself, he slid out of bed, pulled on his discarded pants and strode to the door, opening it a crack.

'Your Highness.' The maid curtseyed, dropping her gaze. 'I'm sorry to intrude. But my lady asked me to bring any package from France to her immediately. She's been waiting for it.'

'That's fine.' He held out his hand. 'I'll give it to her. And you can bring breakfast in half an hour.'

He closed the door, reading the sender's details. Not her sister. His curiosity rose.

'Who was it?' Ghizlan's voice was soft and incredibly seductive with its just awake roughness.

'A package for you, from France.'

'France?' She sat up, excitement in her voice. Huseyn

stood, drinking in the bounty of her beautiful body, until she caught his stare and dragged the sheet up over her breasts. Faint colour tinged her cheeks and throat and he found himself smiling again.

He put the small package in her hands and watched her face light as she ripped it open and worked her way through protective layers. She glowed with excitement and the sight was as enthralling as watching her as she came beneath him, her body slick and welcoming.

'Oh, Jean-Paul!' Her breathy voice cut through Huseyn's thoughts.

'Jean-Paul?'

She didn't answer. Her eyes were closed as she held a small vial to her nose. Her smile was beautiful and infuriating. He didn't want other men making her smile that way.

Huseyn sat down on the bed, hands planted on either side of her hips, forcing her attention back to him.

'Smell this.' She lifted the tiny bottle to his nose and he inhaled, watching the anticipation in her eyes. He smelled sweetness and warmth, something lush and seductive, like the glow in Ghizlan's eyes.

'Roses?'

She nodded. 'And more. It's not overpowering, is it? It's got a delicacy, a freshness that sets it apart.' She bowed her head over the bottle again, her brow pleating in concentration.

'Ghizlan?'

'Hmm?'

'What is it and who's Jean-Paul?' Huseyn was pleased with his even tone. There was no hint of jealousy, though he'd spent too much time wondering about his wife's relationship with both the Frenchman and Idris of Zahrat. He'd never been Ghizlan's choice and the knowledge ate at him, making him wonder if she could ever be truly happy with someone like him. Someone who came from nothing and had fought for everything he had.

'It's a perfume Jean-Paul has developed for me.' She read a note in her hand. There's rose and almond, base notes of vanilla and…ah, that explains the warmth…tonka bean. And—'

'Jean-Paul is a friend?'

What did she read in his expression? Her own changed as she watched him. 'He's a famous "nose". He designs perfumes.'

'And he's been here to Jeirut to design a perfume for your new enterprise?'

She shook her head, ebony hair slipping over her bare shoulders. 'He works from his home in France and I've never met him. We've corresponded.'

'Ah.' Huseyn relaxed and reached for a lock of hair that had slipped towards her cleavage. Her flesh was warm beneath his touch. 'You were so excited I wondered…'

'What? If he was a lover?' Her laughter faded as their eyes met and Huseyn recognised that familiar throb in the air between them. Her eyes widened. 'You *know* I never had a lover before you.'

Soft pink tinged her cheeks and satisfaction slammed into him. Yes, he was primitively possessive where Ghizlan was concerned. Huseyn lifted his shoulders. He refused to apologise.

'The man's in his seventies!'

His hand slid up to cup the fine line of her jaw. 'A man would have to be blind not to want you.'

Her flush turned fiery but the glint of awareness in those dark eyes told him she was thrilled.

'Careful! The perfume! Don't spill it. I need to take it to the factory. We need to name it and discuss production—'

'Ghizlan,' he said against her throat and felt her shiver. 'Call it Ghizlan. It's your scent. Rich and voluptuous but subtle too.'

She pulled back, her eyes round. 'Are you *sweet-talking* me, Huseyn?'

'I've never sweet-talked a woman in my life. I don't do flattery, *my lady*.' He lifted the vial from her hand and placed it carefully on the bedside table. 'I simply call it as it is. Now, why don't you lie there while I wish you good morning properly?'

'You summoned me, my lord?' Ghizlan crossed the echoing throne room where Huseyn had been holding an audience prior to tonight's grand reception.

He turned around, snaring her breath. Even now, after months of intimacy, he did that to her. Even fully clothed. Her gaze skated over his beautifully tailored dinner jacket and down those powerful legs. Something clenched deep inside and she yanked her gaze up. Now wasn't the time. They had a reception in fifteen minutes.

His lazy gaze had turned silver and she knew Huseyn read her expression. She didn't mind one bit.

How times had changed.

'Hardly summoned, *my lady*.' His voice dropped to the low burr that always felt like the slow glide of his hand on bare flesh. It was a lover's voice and she revelled in it. 'I merely asked Azim if he knew where you were.'

He paused, surveying her from head to toe. A smile tilted the corner of his mouth, creating that dimple in one cheek. 'May I say how delectable you look tonight?' He took her hand and turned it over, kissing her palm, then trailing his tongue up to her wrist.

'Huseyn!' It was a gasp of pleasure and shock as she glanced at the closed door. Her nipples budded against her silk evening gown and her skin prickled all over.

'No one will enter without permission.' He drew her closer.

'Because you've warned them not to?' Ghizlan had been surprised and delighted by some of the places they'd made love. Including the stables at midnight after a starlight ride and in their private garden where the setting sun bronzed Huseyn's strong features in the dying light.

'Because no one would interrupt the Sheikh without invitation.' His hands curved round her waist, as always making her feel delicate in his hold.

Ghizlan pressed her hands on his chest, so hard and warm. 'My lipstick,' she murmured as he bent his head. With a sigh he kissed her throat instead, bestowing tiny caresses till she was bowed back in his arms and wished they were anywhere but here, with a crowd waiting for them.

'I want to sweep you off to bed,' he growled, kissing his way past her pearl and tourmaline necklace and heading for her décolletage.

'I want that as well.'

His hands firmed on her waist and he lifted his head, a gleam in his eyes. Ghizlan knew that look.

'No, we can't! We're entertaining the ambassadors of Zahrat and Halarq as part of the peace discussions, remember?'

Huseyn sighed and stepped back. Instantly Ghizlan was bereft. 'It's as well I have you to remind me of my duty.'

She shook her head. That was one thing she'd learned about Huseyn since those early days when she'd thought him brutish and uncivilised. He might be bold and decisive but he took duty seriously. Jeirut couldn't have asked for a better sheikh, albeit one who sometimes struggled to stifle impatience in the face of courtly protocol.

'I have something for you.' He reached behind him and picked up a small, wooden box, beautifully carved.

'It's gorgeous.' She turned the octagonal piece in her hands, marvelling at the delicacy of the work. Each side featured a different flower. As she turned it she recognised each was one being grown locally to supply the perfumery. She traced the curving petals of a perfect rose. Delight filled her at his thoughtfulness. He'd had this made especially. 'Thank you, Huseyn. I'll treasure it. I've never seen work like this before.'

She reached out a hand and his closed around it.

Something beat between them. Something far more than desire. Something solid and comforting and exciting too.

'My province of Jumeah was once known for its crafts-manship, but decades of misrule and threats from across the border all but destroyed our economy. It's only in the last couple of years that there's been a revival.'

Thanks to Huseyn. Not that he'd told her. She'd made it her business to learn about the province that had been a black hole as far as her father was concerned. She'd discovered Huseyn's support was a driving force in turning around the fortunes of his people. She admired him for that.

'I'd like to take you there.' His voice held an unfamiliar gruff note. 'To show you its natural beauty and how the people are starting anew.'

'I'd like that.' She meant it. She wanted to see the place Huseyn had grown up. The place that had moulded him.

'There's more.' His hand squeezed hers then dropped away. 'Open it.'

She lifted the lid and her breath caught. 'It's stunning.' Nestled in a bed of scarlet silk rested the most beautiful piece of glasswork she'd ever seen. 'Also from Jumeah?'

She looked up to read the pride and satisfaction he didn't bother to hide. 'Another ancient art that had all but died. There are only a few old craftsmen left but we've initiated a scheme for them to train the young.'

'If they can create work like this it will be a huge suc-cess.' Carefully she lifted the delicate, unusual piece from its bed and held it to the light. It was a small bottle, its body a swirl of colour from pale gold to apricot, peach and amber, with a hint of scarlet threading through, bringing it to life. Its tall, twisted stopper was of intertwined gold and scarlet.

'Your sister designed it.'

'Mina?' Ghizlan's eyes widened. She'd had no idea Huseyn had been in contact with her.

'She did a wonderful job, don't you think?'

'Marvellous.' Ghizlan cradled the precious piece. 'But I don't understand.'

'Since the flagship scent for your perfumery will be called Ghizlan—'

'That's what *you* want.' She still wasn't sure about naming the scent after herself.

He shook his head. 'Your team agrees wholeheartedly. I heard about the vote.' Ghizlan frowned, wondering how he knew. 'Having you as the face of the scent as well as the business will give it a cachet no other perfume has.'

'Flatterer.'

His mouth kicked up at the corner and he trailed the back of one finger down her cheek, the look in his eyes turning her insides to mush.

'I never flatter. It's the truth.' His gaze held hers so long and with such intensity she felt emotions well far too close to the surface. Tender new feelings she strove not to name, but which grew stronger every day.

Huseyn cleared his throat. 'I told Mina the name of the perfume and asked her to design a bottle for it. Something distinctive.' He smiled. 'Your little sister has genuine talent. See how she took inspiration from your name?' His long finger traced the unusual shape of the glass in her hand. 'Knowing you wanted to market this internationally she used the English language letter Z as her model.'

Ghizlan followed his gesture, recognising the letter shape, sinuous and distinctive in Mina's design. 'It's unlike anything I've ever seen. It's utterly beautiful.'

'It works then?' To her surprise he sounded diffident, almost tentative.

She looked up, meeting an unreadable stare. 'How could it not? Any woman would love to own something as precious as this. If it can be replicated?'

He nodded. 'It can. That was part of the brief.'

'Oh, Huseyn.' Suddenly her hands were trembling and he scooped the delicate piece up and into its box, then placed it on a nearby table.

'Ghizlan? What's wrong? I thought you liked it?'

She blinked, telling herself she was overreacting. 'I love it. I never expected anything like this. That you would take the time to plan something so thoughtful...'

'Because I'm a barbarian brute?' He took her hands in his, his hold firm yet gentle.

She shook her head. She'd discovered he was anything but. She'd learned, as they'd discussed politics, made love, and spent time together, that Huseyn was a complex man of integrity and surprising tenderness despite his authoritative streak. He'd even cajoled her back into the saddle, taking her for rides in the countryside. To her surprise she'd found joy in their marriage and a sense of accomplishment as he encouraged her to pursue her interests as her father never had.

'Because no one has ever given me anything so perfect. So thoughtful. I can't tell you...'

'You don't need to. I know. I felt the same way about those books you gave me.'

Ghizlan's eyes rounded. 'That wasn't at all the same. That was easy—'

He drew her closer, the light in his eyes beacon-bright. 'It was the first gift I've ever received,' he said with a stark simplicity that silenced her. 'It meant everything. It made me want to give you something that meant almost as much.' He leaned in, his breath warm on her face. 'And now I've discovered how good it feels to give, I think I'm addicted. If you could only see how beautiful you look right now.'

Ghizlan's eyes grew misty and her throat closed as happiness and awe filled her. The look in those silvery-blue eyes made her feel...

'Huseyn! My lipstick! We've got guests waiting—'

'To hell with your lipstick. And the guests.' And he proceeded to demonstrate how much she enjoyed that authoritative, downright bossy streak in him.

CHAPTER THIRTEEN

GHIZLAN'S STEP WAS light as she approached the stables. After a day apart, each working on their own projects, she and Huseyn were going riding together. She was early, planning to take him to a secluded grove outside the city, a place she hadn't visited for years. When she'd stopped riding she'd never found time to go back to that tiny valley of green in the stark hills. It had always seemed magical with its drifts of wild purple irises and pink cyclamen. Now she wanted to share it with Huseyn.

Once she'd have baulked at sharing such a special place with him. But her feelings had changed. Sometimes it scared her, how much they'd changed and how big a part he played in her life, not through force but because she wanted him there.

That was what made the difference. No force. Every step they took to a deeper, more meaningful relationship was mutual, her decision as much as his. Because she wanted him. Not just sexually.

Happiness filled her, a lightness she'd never known before. Because of Huseyn.

The only dark cloud, and it was minor, was his steadfast refusal to accept Sheikh Idris's invitation, conveyed through his ambassador, for them to visit Zahrat. Huseyn declared it too soon, because peace talks with Halarq hadn't concluded so he couldn't leave the country. Whereas Ghizlan wanted to see her friend Arden and, she recognised with a smile, to show off her husband.

She reached the stables. Selim was there and greeted her, moving aside so she could see.

She wished she couldn't. For in the centre of the cobbled yard was a scene that took her breath away—Huseyn in riding clothes, looking calm and ridiculously at ease as a dark stallion danced and reared around him.

Huseyn approached with a halter and the horse's lethal hooves flashed. Ghizlan gasped, her hand to her throat as the scene played out—the horse wild and dangerous with its sudden lunges, the man confident and patient.

How long it took, Ghizlan didn't know, but with what looked like consummate ease, Huseyn finally slid the halter on the horse then vaulted onto its back, all the time whispering words she couldn't catch.

'It's like magic,' she breathed as her racing heart began to ease into a normal rhythm. 'I don't know how he does it.'

Selim laughed. 'You're right, he has the gift. But it's not magic. He assesses the horse carefully, a risk assessment, if you like, learning its fears and reactions. Huseyn has always been clever like that, patient enough to take time to see what others don't. And he does care about them, he's always had a soft spot for horses, but, believe me, every step in the process is calculated.'

Ghizlan's gaze narrowed on the powerful man astride the stallion that pranced, not quite docile, beneath him.

Selim spoke again and the words were like tiny shards of ice pricking her suddenly cool flesh. 'Huseyn doesn't give up when he's presented with a challenge. He sets about winning a horse's trust, gentles it until it accepts him, gets used to his presence, even welcomes him. The beauty of it is that when he's finished the animal thinks it's pleasing itself but he's actually taught it to want what he wants, responding to his subtle cues. Make no mistake, he's always the master. But the animal welcomes him.'

Just then the horse reared its head, whinnying and rolling its eyes. It lifted off the ground in a jump designed to unseat its rider and Ghizlan caught the flash of excitement on Huseyn's face as he rode it until it stopped. Its ears flicked back as he leaned forward, whispering soothing words.

So like the whispered praise he murmured in her ear when she accepted him into her body, opened her arms to him, offered herself for his pleasure whenever and wherever he wanted.

A knot of raw emotion, hot and horrible and heavy as the palace's giant foundation stones, pressed down on her chest. It cramped her lungs, pushed her heart to a slow, ominous beat of realisation and betrayal.

Just so had Huseyn made her accustomed to his presence, insisting on sharing a bed, tempting her with that superb body. Had he seen her as a challenge? Of course he had. He'd bragged about all the willing women he'd bedded. Only she had stood up to him. How that must have pricked his pride.

Was that why he'd taken the time to *gentle* her, *tame* her, persuade her that she desired only what he wanted? The single time since he'd seduced her that she'd argued for something *she* wanted—to visit Zahrat—he'd dismissed the idea so quickly she'd wondered at his vehemence.

Because he wants everything his way. What you want doesn't matter unless it fits his plans. He sugarcoats his commands and you eat out of his hand like one of his damned horses.

Ghizlan shrivelled inside, torn between stark horror at the revelation and the wounded part of her that refused to believe it.

But memories flicked through her brain in quick succession, reminding her how patiently he'd searched out her weaknesses and secret desires, then proceeded to give her what she hadn't even known she'd wanted. Tenderness, caring. Acceptance.

He'd given more than she'd ever had from anyone in her life, including her distant father who'd only approved of her when her hard work and dedication had coincided with his own goals. Had it all been a sham?

'My lady? Are you well?'

She blinked and realised she'd slumped against a pillar, her hand splayed on the gritty surface for support.

'I'm...'

Gutted?

Finally seeing my husband for what he is?

And seeing myself, the stupid virgin who believed herself strong but was so easily seduced into compliance.

'I'm fine.' She stiffened her backbone and turned, donning a smile that hurt. 'But I've just remembered something I need to do.'

She turned and marched away, head high, heart bleeding. Only when she was out of sight did she give in to the pain and use the handrail to drag herself up the stairs. It felt as if every bone in her body was bruised.

But the physical pain was nothing to the raw, throbbing ache in her heart.

Slowly she climbed from floor to floor and with each step part of her cried, *It's not true. It's not true.*

And every time another memory surfaced, of Huseyn slowly, carefully worming his way into her world, her affections, giving her praise and tenderness when she hadn't even realised she was needy.

Why had he bothered? It couldn't just be the sex. A man as virile as Huseyn could get that wherever he wanted.

Because she'd thrown down the gauntlet and he'd made it clear he refused to be bested by some 'pampered waste of space'? At the time the words had infuriated rather than hurt. Now she wondered if that was really how he saw her. Did he actually care about the projects she was passionate about, like the perfumery? Or did he encourage her in order to keep her out of his hair while he pursued his own agenda?

Ghizlan frowned. No, that wasn't right. He discussed his

plans with her, got her to help him. Yeah, got her to help him smooth the diplomatic wrinkles. He trotted her out at high powered functions, or when he deemed a woman's charm was useful. She was his ace up the sleeve—born royal, bred to be a hostess, charming and accomplished and useful at negotiating the tangled web of regional politics.

He'd been forced to marry her to win the sheihkdom and he'd decided he might as well get his money's worth.

Ghizlan stopped at the top of the steps to the royal bedrooms and sagged against the wall.

She tried to summon a counterargument. To convince herself she was wrong, but it made too much sense. Everything slotted into place with sickening certainty. Huseyn had deliberately, coldly, seduced her, physically and emotionally. He had her exactly where he wanted her.

Knowing that, she had to break free from him.

A bitter laugh escaped and she shivered at the high, out-of-control sound. She didn't *want* to break free. She enjoyed her gilded cage too much. She tried to tell herself that once she made the break she could follow her own dream for the future, rather than be part of his schemes.

But the dreadful irony was that she didn't *have* a dream for the future. She was living the dream. These last months had been the happiest of her life. The admission scooped her stomach empty.

Despite years trapped in a life driven by duty, she loved what she was doing, now she had the latitude to do it her way and pursue her own interests. There was nothing she wanted more than to see those projects to maturity, to serve her country in ways that best used her skills, and to share her life with Huseyn.

He'd been everything she'd never dared hope for—tender, passionate, challenging, even fun now he'd learned to relax and show the man behind the imposing façade.

Or was that a carefully constructed illusion?

Ghizlan drew an aching breath, facing the ominous truth

that she wanted that man to be real as she'd never wanted anything in her life. Because she'd given not just her body and her trust to him. She'd given her heart too.

With that realisation came pain so deep it was as if her insides were being ripped asunder.

Her breathing ragged, she set her jaw and forced herself to put one foot in front of the other. Soon she'd reach the sanctuary of her apartments.

Their apartments! She no longer even had the privacy of a place to hide and lick her wounds.

Ghizlan's step faltered but she pushed on. One thing at a time. She'd have to find a new haven and a new dream. One that didn't come at the price of her self-respect.

Huseyn's booted feet took the stairs three at a time, impatience riding him. And concern. It had only been after he'd finished working with the new stallion that Selim mentioned Ghizlan had been at the stables early for their ride. And that she'd suddenly looked green around the gills and hurried off.

Ghizlan was never ill. Even when suffering cramps on the first day of her period, she never missed an appointment. But she didn't have her period. This morning she'd straddled him, riding him hard and fast until they'd both collapsed in ecstasy. The memory of her delectable breasts jiggling against his chest, the blaze of delight in her eyes as she climaxed made him tighten anew. It was a position she enjoyed and he was happy to relinquish control of their loving when it gave him the opportunity to watch that shock of rapture overtake her as she milked his body dry.

The thought of her ill sent a niggle of anxiety through his gut.

The other alternative, that she had morning sickness, made him anxious too and triumphant at the same time. Pregnancy wouldn't be surprising, given how insatiable they were for each other. In the beginning he'd wondered if his formidable sex drive would be too much for Ghizlan, especially as it seemed to know no limits when his wife was around. But she was an eager partner. So eager.

The idea of her carrying his child struck at something visceral. An image of Ghizlan blooming with his child made him simultaneously proud, horny and worried as hell.

He pushed open the door to their sitting room and strode to the bedroom, telling himself he was jumping the gun. There was nothing—

An open suitcase lay on the bed.

'Yes, please. That dress and the blue as well. No, not the rest. That's plenty.' Ghizlan's voice came from the walk-in wardrobe.

'Ghizlan?' His voice sounded overloud in the empty bedroom and he found his gaze fixed on the suitcase, already containing a neat stack of clothes.

There was silence for a moment, then she emerged carrying an armful of clothes. She looked pale, too pale. There was a tightness around her lips and a tiny furrow between her brows that spoke of pain. She lay the clothes on the bed as carefully as if they were made of glass, then straightened, her eyes fixed warily on him.

Something shifted in his belly. That stare. He hadn't seen that expression in months. Not since she'd viewed him as the devil incarnate for capturing the palace, and her.

Her maid appeared, bearing dresses on hangers, her gaze darting from her mistress to him.

'Leave us.' He kept his voice steady but still it emerged with a raw, dangerous edge.

Ghizlan's chin lifted. 'We're not finished.'

Oh, they were. They had no trip planned except a visit to his home province of Jumeah next week. And his wife was going nowhere without him.

'Do you really want to have this conversation in front of your maid?'

For an instant longer Ghizlan stood, rigid and unblinking, then she nodded to the maid who placed her burden on the bed and scurried away. Huseyn waited until the outer door shut before closing the space between himself and Ghizlan.

This close he saw a shiver rip through her, and her eyes widen in an expression of distaste.

Huseyn slammed to a stop, a sick feeling in his gullet. 'What the hell is going on?' He hadn't intended the words. Even when he'd seen the suitcase he'd intended to be calm. But seeing his wife look at him like something repellent she'd discovered under a desert rock ate at his good intentions like acid.

She lifted her shoulders in a tight shrug. 'Packing. Even though you can't visit Zahrat, there's nothing stopping me accepting Idris's invitation.'

A red haze misted Huseyn's vision. His fingers curled into tight fists and deliberately straightened them.

'No. You don't leave without me.' It was non-negotiable.

'I *beg* your pardon?' Hauteur turned her features ice cold, a blue-blooded princess outraged by the presence of a rough brute who was more at home in the stables than the royal apartments. 'You don't order me, Huseyn. We agreed I could travel when things had settled.'

She stuck her fists on her hips, destroying the ice princess image and morphing into the passionate, hot-blooded virago who'd driven him to distraction. He was torn between fury and lust. And something else. Something perilously close to fear. After all that they'd shared, she was ready to spurn him?

'So desperate to see him, then?' Bile rose, filling the back of his mouth.

Ghizlan turned and ostentatiously splayed out the dresses that had been dumped on the bed. 'Not so much him, but his wife Arden. She's a friend of mine. And after Zahrat I thought I'd head to Paris to see—'

'The Sheikha is a friend of yours?' Huseyn almost

laughed at how he'd missed the most obvious explanation. 'It's not Idris you've been calling all this time. *She's* your mysterious friend?' He'd tortured himself imagining she had a relationship, even if not a physical one, with Idris. All this time, even when his relationship with Ghizlan had grown so easy, it had been there—a secret shadow marring his contentment, mocking their hard-won closeness.

Ghizlan wheeled, eyes round and mouth open. Then she snapped her teeth shut with an audible click. 'How do you know who I've been calling? Have you been spying on me?' Her stare was as lethal as on the day they'd met.

He stepped closer. 'No. I simply had numbers dialled from the palace monitored in the weeks after I arrived, as a precaution. I didn't know if your staff would respect me as their new Sheikh or try to undermine me while I was away negotiating a peace deal. The report on my return showed calls from your private extension to the palace in Zahrat.'

'And you kept monitoring?' Her gaze kindled.

He nodded, refusing to apologise. Sheer, glorious relief swamped him at the knowledge she wasn't pining for another man. He'd found it hard to believe, especially when they'd grown so close. But the doubt had always been there, taunting him, reminding him he was bastard-born, rough and battle-scarred, the polar opposite of Ghizlan, so refined, elegant and well educated. Would it have been so surprising if his cultured, clever wife had been attracted to a man who'd grown up with the same advantages she had?

'Why?' Curiosity warred with anger in her dark gaze. 'Why not ask me about it? You've never hesitated to confront me before. Why sneak behind my back? Or is that more your style?'

Huseyn frowned. Where had that come from? 'I hoped you'd trust me enough to tell me about it yourself one day.'

Had he? Or had he been scared that if he brought it into the open, made her admit her unrequited feelings for another man, it would be the end of the relationship *he'd* built with Ghizlan?

Huseyn thrust his shoulders back, shaking off the notion. This relationship wasn't ending. He wouldn't allow it.

'Trust you?' Her voice rose to a high, unfamiliar note that worried him. Even at her angriest Ghizlan had never sounded so close to the edge.

He moved nearer and her rapid breathing feathered the V of skin where the neck of his shirt hung open, making his flesh tighten. Never had a woman affected him so easily.

'You thought I was betraying my country by passing sensitive information to another ruler?' Her mouth turned down in an angry pout that notched his belly tight.

'Of course not! You care too much for Jeirut to betray it.'

She stared up at him, her eyes narrowing. 'So you thought it was personal? How many times do I need to tell you there's nothing between me and Idris? It was a dynastic match. The man is head over heels in love with his wife!' She paused, catching her breath. 'And if I had been in love with him, I'd never have told you. Why should I? You and I are nothing but a…a convenient coupling.'

The depth of her scorn seared him, past pride and reason to something far more vital. Emotion pulsed hard, so vehement every muscle contracted as if in readiness for battle.

How could she deny what they had? How dared she?

'Convenient?' His voice was a bass growl, ominous as the thunder preceding the cataclysmic winter storms that occasionally struck the Jeiruti mountains. Storms that tumbled boulders and brought a torrent of white water that could sweep away whole villages in normally dry gullies.

Instinctively Ghizlan backed up a step but huge hands grabbed her upper arms, hauling her so hard against him the air was knocked from her chest.

'You call this *convenient*?' He shook his head, his face

drawn hard and stark as if from pain. 'You're even more innocent than I imagined.'

Then his mouth was on hers, prising her lips apart so he could plunge his tongue deep into her mouth. Her head rocked back with the force of his possession and she clawed at his shoulders, trying to inflict pain and save herself from toppling.

But even as she did, an answering, stormy heat erupted inside her. Ghizlan's tongue met his, lashing and demanding. She sucked him further into her mouth, simultaneously delighting and punishing. Together they felt so good. Even now, when fury and hurt boiled within.

Her body thrummed as electricity struck her breasts, her pelvis, and erogenous zones she hadn't known about.

Then Huseyn's mouth gentled, his hands caressing, as he turned the kiss into something lush and languorous and mind-numbingly tender and Ghizlan found herself powerless to do anything but give him what he wanted. What *she* wanted. A husky sound of masculine pleasure filled her ears and her body relaxed into his embrace. His rock-hard arms gathered her in and his erection pressed, proud and hot against her. She loosened her stance so he could—

No! It was a silent scream against his mouth as she pushed away with all her might.

Hands to his chest, she levered herself away. Knowing she only managed it because he let her made the pain singing in her veins even harder to bear.

'I don't want this.' Even to herself it sounded half-hearted. Because what truly bound her to him wasn't his physical strength but her weakness. The knowledge cut her off at the knees, making her sway in his embrace.

Hot silvery eyes met hers and that silly trembling began along her spine. Surely, if she worked at it long enough, she'd develop an immunity? It was her only hope.

'I thought we'd passed the stage of pretence.' He skimmed one large hand down her side, his thumb brushing in a wide arc below her breast, making her shudder in anticipation of a more intimate touch.

That demonstration of her weakness fuelled both her despair and her determination.

'Let me go, Huseyn.' Her voice was flat.

'Not until you explain.' She said nothing, just stood, shivering in his hold, until he released her, an oath ripping from his mouth. 'Don't look at me like that!'

Ghizlan staggered back to lean against the window alcove, dragging unsteady breaths into lungs that were on fire.

'Are you going to explain?'

'There's nothing to explain. I want to visit Arden in Zahrat and then my sister in—'

'Paris. Yes, I know.' He folded his arms over his massive chest and she was surprised to see how high it rose, as if he found it difficult to breathe too. 'Are you going to tell me what's wrong? Why you're trying to run from me?'

Ghizlan regarded the man who'd become the centre of her world, the reason for her happiness, and considered lying to save face. It hurt that much.

'I discovered what you did.' Emotion throbbed in her voice and she had to pause and swallow. 'I was watching you with that stallion and Selim told me how you worked to tame each one, learning their fears and their foibles, training them to accept you, even *want* your presence. Teaching them to obey your commands, your desires, until they became your creatures...' Her words grew husky and thick and the backs of her eyes prickled but she stared dry-eyed into that silvery-blue stare.

'You enjoy the challenge, don't you? You get your kicks that way, I saw it in your eyes. It's a pity I didn't realise it before.'

'Realise what, exactly?' Not by a flicker did he show a hint of remorse.

Ghizlan stood tall, her chin tilted with all the hauteur

not of a princess but of a woman determined to conquer weakness.

'That you did the same to me. That you saw me as a challenge. You did, didn't you?' There it was, that gleam in his steady stare, betraying him. She'd hit the nail on the head.

'You set about seducing me, calming me, getting me to trust you, to…to *care* for you, like one of your damned horses. You even made me believe—' She snapped her teeth shut before she could reveal how he'd lulled her into thinking he really cared for her.

'Ghizlan…' He reached for her and she put out her arm.

'Don't! Don't touch me.' Her chest was too tight, her throat closing over the words, and raw, tearing pain ripped through her insides. 'You set out to seduce me into caring for you.'

'And if I did?' His jaw tightened. 'If I took the time to try to understand you and give you want you wanted? Is that so bad?' His crossed arms bulged as his muscles bunched and a pulse flicked hard in his jaw. 'What was wrong with respecting your needs and giving you time to make up your mind about me? About trusting you'd come to me eventually?' He shook his head. 'The passion between us was always there, Ghizlan. You can't deny it.'

His expression grew, if anything, harder, his jaw like honed flint. 'Do you think I'd have done that for any other woman?'

Ghizlan stared. 'What are you saying?'

'I told you I don't do flattery. I don't live my life to accommodate any woman.' He lifted one hand, raking his scalp, ruffling his dark hair. 'But that changed with you. *I* changed with you.'

Something danced in his eyes. Something that made her belly tremble and her knees loosen. But she refused to be seduced so easily again.

'You had to change. You realised I had skills and knowledge you could use. How else could you get me to obey when I refused to bow to your every whim?'

Laughter split the air. 'My every whim? That would be the day! You're feisty, stubborn and opinionated, always ready to argue your point of view.'

'All the things you don't want in a woman.' Ghizlan tasted acid on her tongue. She'd thought the hurt couldn't get any worse yet his casual amusement lacerated her.

'I thought you were beginning to know me, Ghizlan.' His voice dropped to a soft note that tugged at her stupid heart. 'Of course I tried to win you over. But you've got it wrong. I didn't do it because I chose to. I did it because I *needed* to.'

Large hands cupped her elbows but that wasn't what welded her to the spot. It was the emotion shimmering in Huseyn's eyes. The ragged note in that deep voice. 'Because I realised long ago that you were more than any woman I'd ever known or expected to know. That you were the only woman I *wanted* in my life.'

Ghizlan's jaw sagged as she met those beautiful, earnest eyes. 'Of course I like it that you can wind ambassadors around your little finger. That you can speak five languages and smooth ruffled diplomatic feathers and act as hostess at a dinner for two hundred. But that's not why I need you.' He paused, dragging in an audible breath as Ghizlan tried not to lean closer.

'I need you because you make me whole. You make me feel like a man I didn't know I could be. A better, kinder man than I've ever been. Is that so bad?'

One long finger stroked her cheek and she swallowed, unable to move, arrested by the words tumbling from those chiselled lips.

'You make me feel things I've never felt before. You make me want what I never expected to want.'

'Like what?' Her voice was as uneven as her pulse. Her skin too tight to contain so much burgeoning emotion.

'Belonging. Love.' He cupped her face in his hands and she melted at what she saw in his face. 'You. I've wanted you so long, Ghizlan. Not just as a necessary bride, but as my lover.'

'I fell into your bed so easily.' She was torn between wanting to believe his words and fearing it was another seduction technique.

'Not easily at all.' His crooked smile made her chest tighten. 'But I don't just mean my lover in bed. It's more than sex I need from you, Ghizlan. I'm greedy. I want you all. Body, heart and soul.' He paused and she heard the throb of her pulse heavy in her ears as she tried to take it in. 'Of course I aimed to seduce you. I wanted you to fall in love with me because I've fallen in love with you. I don't want you dreaming of leaving me for some suave aristocrat who's all the things I'll never be.'

His thumbs stroked her cheeks and Ghizlan realised there was wetness there. Tears she hadn't been aware of spilled from her eyes.

'My darling! It's not that bad, surely? I know I wasn't your original choice but I'd hoped you'd come to care for me too.'

That's when she saw it, the fear in Huseyn's proud, harsh features. It was there in his voice and, if she wasn't mistaken, in the sudden sweat beading his forehead.

This was real. Real and true. A perfect mirror to her own devastatingly raw feelings.

Ghizlan slipped her arms over his warm shirt, over that hard-packed muscle she loved to snuggle against, linking her fingers behind his neck.

'Why didn't you tell me?' The wonder of it almost stole her voice.

'I wanted to bind you to me first. I've never set about seducing a wife before. I wanted to know I'd done it right. Completely and thoroughly so you'd never want to leave.' He paused. '*Then* I was going to tell you.'

Emotion fluttered high in Ghizlan's throat, like a trapped bird.

'You would have saved a lot of trouble if you'd told me.' She paused, overcome by the passion she read in his face and his trembling hands. Who'd have thought those big, capable hands could shake with emotion?

'I thought actions spoke louder than words.'

'So they do.' Her lips curving in a taut smile, Ghizlan rose on tiptoe and dragged his head down, kissing him full on the mouth, lingering but light, for she couldn't afford to get distracted.

He grabbed her round the waist, hauling her close. His eyes blazed brighter than any of the fabulous diamonds in the royal collection.

'Tell me!' It was an order, husky and urgent. Ghizlan revelled in the knowledge he was as desperate as she.

'I love you, Huseyn. I didn't want to but I can't seem to help myself.' She leaned in, her lips on his. Her heart thumped a joyous rhythm that mocked her recent despair.

'When did you—? No, tell me later. We've got all the time in the world to discuss the hows and whys. Right now I want a kiss from my wife—the only woman who will ever hold my heart.'

'Is that a command, my lord?' Somehow Ghizlan found she didn't mind his dictatorial ways.

'It is, my lady.' He swept her up off the floor, cradling her with a gentleness that turned her insides liquid. Ghizlan snuggled close, still stunned by the happiness radiating from her heart and the dazzled look in Huseyn's eyes.

There was nowhere she'd rather be than in her husband's arms.

When they kissed again it was a tender promise of joy to come. A gift offered and accepted. A wondrous, heartfelt vow that would last a lifetime.

EPILOGUE

'So the stories about your husband *were* true.' Arden caught Ghizlan's eye as she sipped iced juice.

'Which stories?' Ghizlan frowned. 'You shouldn't believe rumours.'

Arden chuckled. 'You're so protective, it's cute. Though I've never met anyone who needed protection less.'

Ghizlan leaned back in her seat. 'You're teasing.'

'I am. I like him immensely, especially since he dotes on you. But when we first met I wondered. There was a rumour that he forced you into marriage. And he's such a big man, so powerful, with such an air of determination.' Arden shook her head. '*I* wouldn't like to cross him.'

'Oh, I don't know.' Ghizlan smiled down at her glass. 'It can be quite invigorating.'

Arden giggled. 'I'll bet. Making up with Idris has always been a highlight of our relationship.'

'So it's going well?' Ghizlan barely needed to ask. Arden and Idris clearly adored each other.

'Wonderfully,' Arden breathed, smoothing a hand over her stomach. 'So wonderful we're expecting another baby.'

'Congratulations!' Ghizlan sprang from her seat to embrace her friend. 'I'm so happy for you.'

'Thank you. We're thrilled.' Arden failed to hide her curiosity as her gaze dipped to Ghizlan's flat stomach.

Who knew, perhaps one day soon she and Huseyn would be expecting a baby too. She'd stopped taking the Pill, so nature could take its course.

'There they are now.' Arden frowned. 'Though I'm still not sure Dawud's old enough for a pony.'

Huseyn led a pony across the palace courtyard, talking

gently to both the animal and the small boy on its back. Idris walked behind, ready to support his son if necessary.

They stopped and the boy turned to Huseyn for help getting down. It shouldn't surprise her. Dawud had been fascinated by him ever since she and Huseyn had arrived in Zahrat. And her husband, despite that air of formidable power, was easy and infinitely patient with him.

'I've been ousted in my son's affections,' Idris complained as he kissed his wife.

'I'm just a novelty.' Huseyn's laugh rolled through Ghizlan, low and appealing, turning her bones liquid. He walked closer, the boy tucked easily in his arm, and Ghizlan was struck by how natural he was with Dawud. How easily he'd take to fatherhood when the time came.

Huseyn's gaze lifted as if he read her thoughts. Heat pulsed between them as those misty blue eyes snared hers.

'Here. You'd better let me take him.' Idris reached for his boy. 'Before you forget he's there.'

Huseyn relinquished Dawud with a smile and sank to the grass at Ghizlan's feet. 'Good idea. My wife is far too distracting.' He took her hand and pressed his lips to her palm, sending darts of delight through her.

'In that case, Ghizlan, perhaps you can join us for the trade negotiations. I'm for anything that will give Zahrat an advantage. Your husband's a tough negotiator.'

Huseyn beamed at her in a way *she* found utterly distracting. 'Good idea. Ghizlan is my secret weapon. She'll negotiate us into a better position than I could.' His voice softened meaningfully and his eyes gleamed. 'Which would give us reason to celebrate.'

'Ha! Save us from newlyweds!' Idris laughed.

'Actually…' Huseyn kissed her hand again, then turned to the man Ghizlan knew he already liked and respected. 'If Ghizlan agrees, I've been thinking it would be an excellent idea for her to take the lead in some of the discussions.'

Her eyes rounded but he ignored her shock. 'She was the

architect behind the innovative trade schemes and no one knows more about the joint power proposals.' He turned to her. 'If you'd like to, of course. I know you're going to be busy with the launch of the new perfume.'

Ghizlan stared. It was one thing to support Huseyn behind the scenes. This would break every unwritten law—allowing a woman such an important, public role in the nation's future. Yet his gaze told her he was serious.

'Say yes.' His tone was urgent. 'I want you by my side where you deserve to be. You're more than my wife and lover, you're my partner, my other half. I want everyone to see how important you are, to Jeirut and to me.'

Dimly, Ghizlan was aware of Arden's sigh but she couldn't tear her gaze from Huseyn's. Her heart tumbled as she read warmth, pride and love, above all love, in his eyes. 'The Council will have fits.'

'As if I care. With you beside me we can do anything. It's time our people saw you as you really are: my equal.'

'Oh, Huseyn.' She cupped his face, uncaring of their audience. 'You make me so happy.'

'Excellent.' He leaned in to murmur against her ear, 'That's my long-term goal. To make you so happy you'll always love me the way you do now.' His arm went around her waist as he turned to their host. 'You'd better beware, Idris. My Ghizlan's a force to be reckoned with.'

'I think the pair of you are.'

He was right, Ghizlan knew. Together, she and Huseyn were as perfect a match as love could make. She counted herself the luckiest woman ever, knowing he'd always be there beside her, no matter what the future held.

* * * * *

MILLS & BOON®

EXCLUSIVE EXTRACT

Persuading plain Jane to marry him was easy
enough – but Shiekh Zayed Al Zawba hadn't
bargained on the irresistible curves hidden under
her clothes, or that she is deliciously untouched.
When Jane begins to tempt him beyond his
wildest dreams, leaving their marriage
unconsummated becomes impossible...

Read on for a sneak preview of
THE SHEIKH'S BOUGHT WIFE

It was difficult to be *distant* when your body seemed to
have developed a stubborn will of its own. When she found
herself wanting to push her aching breasts against Zayed's
powerful chest as he caught her in his arms for the traditional first dance between bride and groom. As it was, she
could barely think straight and wasn't it the most infuriating
thing in the world that he immediately seemed to pick up
on that?

'You seem to be having trouble breathing, dear wife,'
he murmured as he moved her to the center of the marble
dance floor.

'The dress is very tight.'

'I'd noticed.' He twirled her around, holding her back
a little. 'It looks very well on you.'

She forced a tight smile but she didn't relax. 'Thank you.'

'Or maybe it is the excitement of having me this close
to you which is making you pant like a little kitten?'

'You're *annoying* me, rather than exciting me. And I do
wish you'd stop trying to get underneath my skin.'

'Don't you like people getting underneath your skin, Jane?'

'No,' she said honestly. 'I don't.'

'Why not?'

She met the blaze of his ebony eyes and suppressed a shiver. 'Does everything have to have a reason?'

'In my experience, yes.' There was a pause. 'Has a man hurt you in the past?'

This was her chance to tell him yes—even though the very idea that someone had got that close to her was laughable.

Zayed had already guessed she might be a virgin, but that didn't even come close to her shameful lack of experience.

Trying to ignore the way his groin was brushing against her as he edged her closer, she glanced up at him, her cheeks burning. 'I refuse to answer that on the grounds that I might incriminate myself. Tell me instead, do you always insist on interrogating women when you're dancing with them?'

'No. I don't,' he said simply. 'But then I've never had a bride before and I've never danced with a woman who was so determined not to give anything of herself away.'

'And that's the only reason you want to know,' she said quietly. 'Because you like a challenge.'

'All men like a challenge, Jane.' His black eyes gleamed. 'Haven't you learned that by now?'

She didn't answer—because how was she qualified to answer any questions about what men did or didn't like?

Don't miss
THE SHEIKH'S BOUGHT WIFE
By Sharon Kendrick

Available May 2017
www.millsandboon.co.uk

Join Britain's BIGGEST Romance Book Club

- **EXCLUSIVE offers every month**

- **FREE delivery direct to your door**

- **NEVER MISS a title**

- **EARN Bonus Book points**

Call Customer Services
0844 844 1358*

or visit
millsandboon.co.uk/subscription.